CHICO'S CHALLENG

THE STORY OF AN

AMERICAN QUARTE

Jessie Haas

Feiwel and Friends • New York

Received On
MAY -- 2013
Magnolia Library

A Feiwel and Friends Book
An Imprint of Macmillan

 Printed in the United States of America
by Quad/Graphics, Fairfield, Pennsylvania. For information,
address Feiwel and Friends, 175 Fifth Avenue, New York, N.Y. 10010.

Library of Congress Cataloging-in-Publication Data Available

ISBN: 978-0-312-66680-4

Book design by Barbara Grzeslo

Feiwel and Friends logo designed by Filomena Tuosto

First Edition: 2012

10 9 8 7 6 5 4 3 2 1

mackids.com

Dear Reader,

Welcome to the Breyer Horse Collection book series!

When I was a young girl, I was not able to have a horse of my own. So, while I dreamed of having my own horse one day, I read every book about horses that I could find, filled my room with Breyer model horses, and took riding lessons.

Today, I'm lucky enough to work at Breyer, a company that is known for making authentic and realistic portrait models of horse heroes, great champions, and of course, horses in literature. This beautiful new fiction series is near to my heart because it is about horses whose memorable stories will take their place alongside the horse books that I loved as a child.

This series celebrates popular horse breeds that everyone loves. In each book, you'll get to appreciate the unique characteristics of a different breed, understand their history, and experience their life through their eyes. I believe that you'll love these books as much as I do, and that the horse heroes you meet in them will be your friends for life.

Enjoy them all!

Stephanie Macejko

Breyer Animal Creations

CHAPTER 1

THE YOUNG BUCKSKIN QUARTER HORSE stood perfectly still as the needle slid into his neck. One black-tipped ear tilted back. "Good boy, Chico," the vet said. She pressed the plunger and withdrew the needle.

That would be the last shot, Chico knew. He'd now been through this four times, once for each year of his life. Every year, just as the spring grass would begin to smell unbearably fresh and good, this woman would come. Each horse would be led out of the paddock in turn–Chico's mother, sister, older brothers, and finally him. The vet would look him over, then sting him like a fly, once in each haunch and once on the neck. Other than the stings, she was quiet and pleasant, and like most people, she admired Chico. He could tell by the tone of her voice, though he didn't understand all the words.

As the needle slid out of Chico's neck muscle this time, the vet reached into her pocket, and Chico nickered. The last sting was always followed by a carrot, or once, an apple–

Carrot this year. Good. Chico crunched it, nodding his head with every bite. His life had too much sameness, but this kind of sameness he liked.

Any other year Dean, his owner, would unsnap the cross-ties and lead Chico back to where his family gathered at the round-bale feeder in the barren, packed-earth paddock, swishing their tails, feeling the warmth and shove of each others' bodies, listening to the peaceful crunch of hay and their own slowing heartbeats. They calmed down more quickly with Chico there. The youngest, he was also the bravest. A young male's job in every horse herd was to investigate threats and drive them off. Chico charged into this task with zest. He challenged blowing sheets of newspaper and aimless umbrellas fearlessly, and his greatest joy was driving out stray dogs that wandered into the paddock. That didn't happen often enough. He needed a bigger job–a bigger *life*!

But today, instead of leading Chico back to his family, Dean stood talking with the vet and the girl she'd brought with her.

The girl didn't seem to be listening to the grown-ups talk. A slim teenager with dark curls springing out from under her cowboy hat, she hung back and didn't say much, just gazed at Chico with shining eyes. She was excited. He could feel it.

But what did it have to do with him? He looked out the open barn door, past the girl, past the vet's truck and the horse trailer she'd brought this time, smelling and listening for what lay beyond.

Past Dean's suburban ranch house was another just like it, surrounded by grass instead of dirt and horse fence. Past that was another house, and another, in all directions.

But beyond the houses–Chico's nostrils flared as he tested the wind. Beyond was a vastness, an enormous stretch of grass. Early spring was when he could smell it most.

The grass out there was different. It had a wild, pungent scent. Out there was a big sky and animals of some kind–grass-eaters, many grass-eaters, and meat-eaters, too, the wild dogs Dean called "coyotes," which sometimes slunk through the neighborhood. Chico had never seen the vast grassland, but it filled his mind, exciting to think of, impossible to reach.

His whole life had been this five-acre Laramie, Wyoming, ranchette, with its bare paddock. Dean took good care of his horses. There was hay and cool water. There was a round pen with a deep sand footing, where he had taught Chico to be ridden–and that was about all.

Once or twice a week, Dean trailered Chico to a big indoor riding arena and rode him. That should have been interesting. But Dean just raced Chico in circles, and got upset.

Chico liked going fast and stopping fast–but, after a while, what was the point? They never got anywhere, just went around and around in the same old patterns. Boring, but Dean got angry when Chico thought of shortcuts. Then they'd both come home grumpy.

"I've got too many horses and not enough money," Dean was telling the vet, "and I've soured this one on reining." He gave Chico an apologetic pat. "My fault–he's so athletic. He's always seemed like a horse that needed a job, but running patterns isn't real enough for him. I mean–a cowboy doesn't run patterns. He works. But I'm no cowboy, just an amateur breeder who wants to do some showing on weekends and–anyway, bottom line, if you'd take him in a trade against my vet bill, I'd be most grateful."

The vet turned and walked thoughtfully around Chico, as if she'd never seen him before. In a way she hadn't. It was just this past winter that Chico had really grown into himself. At two, his hind legs were longer than his front legs. At three, he'd looked nice, but unfinished.

Now, through the loosening winter hair, it was possible to see what a fine quarter horse he'd become; about fifteen hands, muscular, well-balanced, with a handsome, self-confident head and wise eyes. His body was the color of buckwheat honey, his mane and tail and legs coal black–and splashed up each leg, as if he'd galloped through milk, was a long white stocking. A white blaze made a lightning streak down the middle of his face.

The vet said, "It's one of the top ten rules you learn in vet school. Never accept an animal in payment of a bill!"

Dean made one of his pretending-I'm-not-worried noises.

"But," she went on, "if you have a thirteen-year-old daughter, you understand that rules change!"

"The horses are my kids," Dean said, "and I guess you're right!"

"We've just started looking for a horse for Sierra," the vet said. "Her little sister is pushing to inherit the quarter pony, and we had to put our nice gelding down this spring–" She cleared her throat. "Anyway, Sierra wants to get into cutting–"

Dean said, "Chico's never even seen a cow!"

"But he's got great bloodlines," the girl said suddenly. Chico had almost forgotten she was there. "I mean–his grandmother was a champion, right? I looked his pedigree up online," she explained, sounding a bit embarrassed.

Her mother said, "Our neighbor–Misty Lassiter–has offered to help Sierra bring a horse along. Maybe you've heard of her–she's a top cutting horse trainer."

"That's great," Dean said, looking at Sierra. "I've been trying to make Chico into a reining horse, because–hey, I don't care if it *is* Wyoming! This is a suburb. Do you see any cows around here? But maybe he wants to be a cutting horse like his grandma. Want to take him for a spin?"

Sierra nodded, and Dean saddled Chico. They all went out to the round pen and Sierra mounted.

No one but Dean had ever gotten onto Chico before. The horse turned his head to sniff Sierra's foot, just to make sure he wasn't imagining this. No, she was up there all right!

She was small and light, and they spent a long time adjusting the stirrups for her. Then it was circles–pretty much all you could do in a round pen was circles. Walk, jog, lope.

Sierra asked, "Could I take him out on the street?"

"Sure." Dean opened the gate. Sierra pointed Chico out the driveway and along the flat street, past the backyards, houses, shrubs, and dogs that he knew so well. Chico enjoyed the *clip-clop* of his own hooves on pavement, and the sights; laundry, cats, cars, bikes. Right turn, right turn, right turn, right turn, and he was back at his own driveway. Sierra got off.

"Well?" her mother asked, and then laughed. "Dumb question! I can see it in your eyes!" She turned to Dean. "All right. I'll take Chico in cancellation of your outstanding vet bill, and we'll see if we can turn him into a cutting horse."

Dean slumped in relief. "You'll like him a lot. He's as

steady as they come. He's just too much horse for a little place like this."

For a while they were busy signing papers. Then the vet led Chico to the strange trailer.

He always walked right onto his own trailer, but Chico stopped to think about getting onto this one. It had open slats in the sides. That was different. It smelled like some unfamiliar animal–the same beyond animals Chico often smelled on the wind. It was a warm, heavy, sweet scent–definitely of a grass-eater. Was one of the animals still lurking in there? Did they really expect him to go in with it? Chico braced his front hooves just outside the trailer door. Ignoring the vet's gentle pull on his halter and Dean's firm hand pushing on his butt, he snuffed the air deeply.

There was hay in the trailer, too. Good hay. It smelled wild, like flowers and wind and sky, and it made Chico feel hungry all over. But if the animal was in there–

"Sierra," the vet said. "Go open the other side door so he can see."

In a moment, golden sunlight flooded the trailer, and Chico saw that it was empty, except for a full hay net hanging at the front. He stepped one foot up, then another. The hollow sounds inside were the same as in Dean's trailer. The wall slats made it airier and not as dark. In a moment, Chico was all the way in, tearing his first mouthful of hay out of the net. The grasses were fine-stemmed, fragrant, perfectly cured. He snatched a second bite, noticing in a distant way that they had fastened the butt-chain, clipped the trailer ties onto his halter, closed the back door and one side door.

"All set?" Dean came to the front of the trailer. "I'll miss you." He tried to pat Chico's blaze. Chico pushed past him for another grassy mouthful.

"Hey!" Dean said, catching him by the halter for a moment. "You're getting a second chance here, kid, and those don't come along every day. Don't blow it!"

. . .

THE TRUCK ROLLED SMOOTHLY UP THROUGH the hills toward the Medicine Bow Mountains. Mom drove carefully, glancing often in her side mirror. Sierra stared straight ahead, dazed and unfocused. Three days ago, having her own quarter horse was just a dream. Three days ago, she'd been wondering if Queenie, the quarter pony at home she'd learned to ride on, could possibly be *her* cutting horse. Then Dean called Mom, suggesting this trade. Sierra had spent every spare moment since then online, researching Chico's pedigree and watching cutting videos–especially Misty Lassiter's.

Misty was the reason for all of this. Sierra had seen her first cutting competition only last fall, at Misty's place, and suddenly understood that she lived next door to a champion. From the crown of her big hat to the worn tips of her cowboy boots, Misty was a Wyoming cowgirl, hard-working, down-to-earth, pretty, young, and tough. Not until she saw Misty's lounge full of trophies did Sierra understand that Misty was also a rock star in the cutting world.

Sierra was just starting to be proud to be a fourth-generation rancher. If only she could be useful in Dad's one-man ranch operation. She'd always loved horses, but she was ready for something a little more challenging than trail riding. Cutting was the answer to both wishes. With an offer of training help from Misty, all she needed was a horse. And now she had one.

What would Misty say when she saw Chico? She'd be impressed, of course. How could she not be? "Bring him over and we'll start training," she'd probably say. Beyond that–she'd hang the ribbons she and Chico would come to win on the wall opposite her bed, Sierra decided, so they'd be the first thing she saw every morning. And if–no, when–they won a silver championship belt buckle, she'd wear it every day, like it was no big deal.

. . .

THE HAY WAS GONE, EVERY FRAGRANT WISP, AND now Chico smelled snow on the early-spring air, and pine and mountain flowers.

The trailer was still climbing. The truck engine sounded loud, and the floor under Chico sloped, up and up, and sometimes steeply down, around sharp curves. The unknown-animal smell was strong again.

The truck slowed and turned, and Chico recognized the sound it made when it was going to stop. About time! He banged one hoof against the trailer wall. That usually brought Dean back to check on him, but nothing happened this time.

The tires crunched over gravel, a dog barked, and a young girl shouted, "Mom! You guys took *forever*!"

"An hour longer than usual," Sierra's mother said. "We were pulling a horse trailer."

Everything came to a stop. The stillness felt beautiful for an instant. Then Chico banged the trailer wall again, and whinnied. *Get me out of here! I have to pee!* He had never peed in a trailer before and he didn't want to start now. Too splashy!

"It's all right, Chico, we're coming," Mom said. A moment later, the doors opened. Chico looked past Sierra and her mother. He saw the young girl, a stocky, big-eared dog, a man in a cowboy hat, a rail fence–

"Wow!" the girl said. "He's *beautiful*!"

"He may be upset," Mom said, appearing beside Sierra. "He's never taken a long trailer ride before." She snapped a lead rope into Chico's halter. "Addie, are you out of the way? All right, Sierra."

The chain behind Chico released, and he backed out of the trailer, curving his neck to see over his shoulder even before his four feet touched the ground.

So much *space*! So much sky! This was what he'd always sensed, out beyond. Behind the house and behind the pastures, the trees marched up the sides of sharp-toothed mountains, strong, rocky, and splashed with snow.

Here in the yard, everything was made of logs; log house, log barn, a maze of log corrals–

A horse whinnied. Chico swiveled his head. In one corral, a small mare craned her neck to reach over a gate. She greeted Chico. *Who are you?*

Chico whinnied back. *Who are* you*?*

He wanted to charge over and greet her. He wanted to prance and dance and wiggle, shake the fidgets out of his legs. But Dean had taught him not to do that with a human attached to his halter. Chico made himself stand still and sent a loud whinny ringing out across the pasture.

An unfamiliar rectangular shape lifted its head.

It was an animal! They were *all* animals!

After a moment, several of them came sauntering toward him. They were small in the distance, and he couldn't tell what they might be–but not horses. Definitely not horses.

Vaguely he sensed Sierra coming closer, holding out the flat of her hand near his muzzle. Quickly, politely, he pushed his nose into her palm for a second. She said something. He couldn't hear it because the animals were getting closer. They were much bigger than he'd realized–monstrous beasts. Their hooves rumbled. One stuck its tail in the air, a thin ropy tail with a brush on the end, and shook its head. There were . . . *things* on its head, white curving sticks–

"Mom!" Sierra said. "I can hear his *heart* beating!"

"Step back, Sierra," Mom said. "This Wyoming quarter horse is about to meet his first cow!"

CHAPTER 2

THE BEAST WAS RIGHT THERE ON THE OTHER side of the fence, and okay, that *looked* like a strong fence, but not as strong as this Beast. Chico stared in horror at its horns, its broad, moist muzzle, the long, pointed tongue that came out and licked– Oh, disgusting! Its tongue went all the way up its nostril!

It shook its head, leaving a long stream of glistening saliva on the air. Too much! Chico's feet danced–yet somehow he kept slack in the lead rope, kept himself from pushing into Sierra's mother. Dean had taught him to be careful around people–but please! Couldn't the vet get him out of here?

She didn't seem to think of that. Chico braced on widespread legs and blasted a snort at the Beast. Was it slightly impressed? It lowered its head and gazed at him through its long lashes, until Sierra stepped forward, waving her hat. Then it turned away. Brave girl! But she was obviously upset too; all of a sudden, her smile was gone.

Now that the Beast had stepped back a bit, Sierra's

mother led Chico away from the fence. He followed her, hunching his hindquarters, clamping his tail, trying to see over his shoulder all the way through the gate into one of the log corrals. The chestnut mare was in the next one over. She pushed her head between the bars and whinnied again.

Chico barely noticed. The gate closed behind him, the halter came off his head, and Sierra's mother stepped out of the way. He was free to whirl and stare at the Beast.

It raised its head and gazed at him. It had huge, dark, suspicious eyes, and its hooves were cloven, not round like a horse's. The Beast lifted its tail and–*plop, plop, plop*–deposited a puddle of steaming manure. A *puddle*! What kind of animal pooped like that? What on earth *was* this thing? Chico circled. Sierra said something in a worried voice.

"You can't expect a horse raised in a Laramie backyard to know what to do with a cow," her mother answered soothingly. "He's in culture shock. Give him time."

Their voices came to Chico as if from behind a windowpane. More important to him were the strange animal and other shapes scattered across the plain. So many of them. He barely noticed the hay Sierra tossed into the rack, though the delicious scent drew him unthinkingly closer. When he got near, a low shape startled him and he leaped back.

Sierra said, "Now he's scared of a *water tub*?"

"This is a big day in his life, Sierra. He's just left everything he's ever known. He'll settle down–"

The mare neighed again, so shrilly this time that she pierced the fog of Chico's fear. *I said, Come here!*

She was older. She was a mare. Maybe she was in charge. Chico trotted over to her. Arching their necks, the two horses mingled their breaths, nose to nose, forehead to forehead.

The mare let out a tremendous, deep bellow. *QUEEN! I am QUEEN!* At the same time, she struck out with one front foot, narrowly missing the fence.

Something inside Chico relaxed at that. This was like home. There his mother was queen. She rarely had to say so. All her children had been raised to understand it. If there was a queen here, too, then maybe things would be all right. Chico squealed and struck out, too, just to show that he wasn't a total pushover. Then he pressed his face close to the mare's again. Her sweet horse breath washed over him. *Normal.* Normal seemed so good right now.

After a few more sniffs, the mare turned away, as if she'd seen all she could stand of him. Chico followed her along the fence line, discovering as he did that the low shape was only a tub, with water in it. He was thirsty, but too keyed up to drink. He nosed the hay in the rack; just like what he'd had in the trailer. He took a wisp. Then one of the Beasts moved, out on the plain. Chico jerked his head up and let the hay fall.

"Do you think he'd settle down more quickly if they were in together?" Sierra asked.

Her mother considered. "Good idea. He's used to being with other horses, and he's used to being the youngest in a herd. Queenie should be able to boss him around just fine." She drew back the bars of the gate.

The mare trotted through, neck arched and tail carried high. Chico stood stock-still near the hayrack. The mare came close, and they sniffed and squealed and struck again.

Queen!

Yes, you're the queen.

Queen! Queen!

You bet!

His new queen was three inches shorter than Chico, with hollows over her eyes and patches of grizzled hair at the corners of her mouth. Little. Old.

Queen!

Chico let the Queen drive him from the hay. That brought him near the water tub, and suddenly he *did* feel like drinking. Four deep swallows–it was sweet water, cold water. She drove him from that, too, just like his bossy older sister would have done.

Chico took a deep breath and let it out in a sigh. He felt much better, much. He sauntered into the other corral for a look-see. The mare pursued him at a walk, ears flat back.

At the edges of his vision, Chico sensed the man, the young girl, the dog, coming closer. "Funny!" the man said. "Is she chasing him, or is he leading her around?"

"He's pretty," Addie said. "But Queenie's prettier."

The dog made a disapproving bark. Too much fuss. The horses should shut up.

Chico explored along the fence line, sniffing. There was the scent of another horse, but not fresh. That horse hadn't been around in quite some time. He paused when he came to the toes of a pair of cowboy boots. He raised his head and looked at Sierra, sitting on the top rail. She smiled, then frowned. She smelled upset, and still excited, and maybe a little scared–just like Chico.

Feeling that way himself was bad enough. He didn't want to hang around a human who felt the same way. Besides, the queen was probably about to bite him in the butt. Chico moved on.

Someone put in a second pile of hay, but by dusk that wasn't necessary. The two horses munched side by side. The queen ate with her head down. Chico's head popped up at every mouthful. As he chewed, he gazed across the darkening plains. He smelled the wild, the grass, the snow, the vastness.

But he also smelled the Beasts. They moved. They ate the grass. Sometimes they bellowed uncouth noises, like trucks or motorcycles, across the great distances. Then Chico was glad for the warmth of the mare beside him, the sound of other chewing besides his own.

. . .

SIERRA COULD HAVE DONE WITH A LITTLE LESS closeness. At supper, the whole family seemed to be looking at her, and pretending not to. Even Addie, clopping a horse model across her plate, seemed to have noticed something wrong.

Sierra wished she could put a good face on this. If she could just say something light and casual, about *anything*! But no words came. She caught Mom and Dad exchanging questioning glances. Dad opened his mouth to say something. Mom shook her head, so slightly the motion was almost invisible. He sat back, looking baffled, then said, "He sure is a good-lookin' horse."

Sierra nodded, staring into space.

Suddenly the beeper on Mom's belt went off. With a well-practiced sigh, Dad reached for Mom's plate and cut her steak with swift slices of his knife. He got a plastic container and scooped the steak bites into it. Meanwhile, Mom took her phone to the window and listened.

"Uh-huh . . . Uh-huh. Uh-huh . . . Okay, I'm on my way–have him keep pressure on that leg." She beeped the phone off and turned, just as Dad snapped the lid shut on the plastic container and handed it to her.

"Thanks. It's Misty–a coyote got into the goats. It's a stitching job." She banged out the front door.

Dad said, "Sierra, run after her. Tell her to eat that steak before it gets cold."

Sierra bolted out the front door. She heard a small squeal from the horse corral as the mare asked Chico: *Who's queen?*

"Mom!" she said. The truck was starting, lights coming on. Sierra pounded the driver's side door. "*Mom!* Dad says–"

The window rolled down. "Eat it before it gets cold," Mom said with her mouth full.

"Mom, don't . . . say anything to Misty yet. Okay?"

Mom stopped chewing, maybe stopped breathing for a second. She swallowed audibly. "All right, if that's the way you want it."

Sierra stepped back while Mom turned the truck. The headlights shone for a moment on the horses. Sierra saw Chico's lightning-streak blaze, his curiously pricked ears. For a second, her heart lightened. What a handsome horse!

But how can he be a cutting horse when he's afraid of cows?

Sierra went indoors, bypassing the kitchen on the way

to her room. By the soft light from the hall, she gazed at the Misty Lassiter pictures on her bulletin board.

Carefully sliced from magazines, they showed Misty on a bay horse, a chestnut, a palomino, facing down a cow. Each horse looked different. Some worked the cow with ears pricked intently forward. Others pinned their ears in a threatening expression. Some crouched so low, Misty's boot nearly scraped the ground; their front legs sweeping out in front of them. Others worked more upright.

Misty looked the same in all of them–serious, alert, deeply focused–at one with the horse beneath her and the cow in front of her. She dressed plainly, usually in a dun yellow shirt almost the same color as Chico, a brown cowboy hat, and chaps. In most pictures, the fringe of her chaps stood straight out, snapped to one side by the wind or the horse's turning. And she usually wore a broad silver belt buckle, a trophy from one or another of her championship rides.

Would Sierra ever do that on Chico? A few hours ago she'd been sure of it. Now doubt gnawed at her.

Physically, he was everything a working quarter horse should be. So athletic! Look at the way he'd tried to dodge that cow. But that was exactly backward. He was supposed to make the *cow* dodge. How could Chico do that if cows terrified him?

How come Mom didn't get the problem? She had just kept chattering on about what a nice horse Chico was–what a *brave* horse he was, for heaven's sake! How could she be so blind?

Maybe she couldn't afford to see what was happening. Though no money had changed hands, Chico didn't come free. Dean had owed Mom's vet practice a lot of money, and money was hard to come by on a backcountry cattle ranch, even for a veterinarian. Taking a horse instead of cash was a sacrifice.

So it had to work, Sierra told herself. It just *had* to.

She wished she felt more hopeful.

CHAPTER 3

ALL THE NEXT DAY, CHICO OBSERVED HIS wide, new world. He'd never seen this much space all at once. What lay over the horizons? His senses told him more meadows, more horizons, on and on almost forever. It all felt perfectly right.

Except for the Beasts. No stretch of grass was free of them. Once, a large one and a very small, wobbly one came out of the pines. All the other Beasts trotted toward those two, and the large one shook the two sticks on its head at them. The sticks looked menacing. Deep in his bones, Chico knew they were dangerous. The bellows of the Beasts reached the horse corral, where the queen, Chico noticed, paid absolutely no attention. She didn't even flick an ear toward the commotion.

Well. That was information.

In the afternoon, Sierra's father started up a small motor vehicle. The engine sound felt homelike to Chico. He knew the sounds of all the lawnmowers, cars, and trucks on his old street, especially Dean's.

The four-wheeler started across the meadow. The dog sat beside Dad on the passenger seat, with a smug set to its ears.

Across the meadow, all the Beasts turned and streamed toward the vehicle. The four-wheeler stopped. Dad got out and took something out of the back, which he spread on the ground. The Beasts stood watching with lowered heads, while the dog stalked up and down in front of them. Only when man and dog were back on the vehicle did they surge forward to eat.

Kind of wimpy, then? Chico watched the Beasts eat and disperse; watched them every one of his waking moments, in fact, and even opened his eyes from sleep to watch them again.

In the morning, Sierra and her mother came down to the corral. They caught the horses and tied them near each other, and Sierra brushed Chico. He listened with his whole body. Sierra's hands were soft and fluttery. Chico stood rock still, as Dean had taught him, and as he'd learned in his family herd. That always calmed the others, and it calmed Sierra, too. After a bit, her hands became stronger and smoother, and her breath relaxed. "Good boy," she murmured.

Chico knew that. He'd always been a good boy, until Dean started riding him in circles. Even then, he'd tried.

After brushing came a saddle, different from Dean's. It felt strange on Chico's back, and he turned to sniff the stirrup fender, while Sierra and her mother looked at the saddle and asked each other if it fit him.

Then Sierra tightened the girth, tactfully, like Dean did, a bit at a time. She put Chico's own bridle on him from back home. At the well-known feel and smell of it, he let out a sigh, and Sierra glanced at him quickly. "You like that?" She seemed like a perceptive girl.

"Do you want me to ride him first?" her mother asked. "He might be a little different here."

"I'll do it." Sierra's voice sounded tight.

She mounted, and though it was a stretch, and she had to haul herself up, she barely made the saddle shift. Chico tossed his head. She was so young and light. He'd have to be careful of her.

He waited for some signal as to what she wanted, but she just sat there. "Squeeze again," her mother said.

Chico felt a slight pressure against his sides. Evidently, she wanted him to move, but her legs were shorter than Dean's, and her signals hard to detect. He stepped forward, one ear tilted to listen to Sierra. Hopefully she wouldn't ask for any stupid circles.

Once, twice around the corral. He felt her start to relax, and he relaxed, too. *Jog? Sure thing.* He had a loose, easy jog, and Sierra's body moved fluidly along with it.

Now she wanted a turn. She put the rein against his neck, and Chico made a decision. Lately, when Dean had put the rein on him, he wanted a fast turn, a sharp turn, something very precise. But when he'd first started riding Chico, any old turn had been good enough. If Chico changed directions at all, Dean was happy.

Those were better days, before all the circles. Now Chico was starting fresh with a new rider; it was a good time to set some ground rules.

He turned, rather lazily. Dean would have let out an exclamation of disgust; would have made him do it again. But Sierra said, "Wow! He's so much quicker than Queenie!" She rode Chico in some squiggles and circles at the jog. Then she asked for a lope. Chico took up a gentle, rocking-horse gait. Dean would have criticized it. Sierra said again, "Wow!"

"I'm glad to hear you say that!" Mom said. "And you know, he'll get over his fear of cows. Give the poor town boy a little time!"

"Mmm." For some reason Sierra stiffened up again, but not as badly.

Mom mounted the queen, and they rode out into the yard. It was bigger than Dean's whole street! Addie waved from the porch. The dog sat beside her, watching critically. Chico could tell that it didn't like him. *Too bad! Try straying into that horse corral, mutt!* He put a show-offy twinkle into his heels, and Sierra gently checked him. "Walk."

Side by side, the two horses went down the ranch road. Log fences gave way to wire. Beasts dotted the grassland–which smelled even more tempting today, Chico noticed. The spring sun was bringing new growth, and the Beasts, heads down, were all wolfing it down. *Not fair!* He jigged in protest and tossed his head, getting half a length ahead of the queen, who nipped him on the shoulder.

The brown ribbon of road stretched to the far horizon, and when they got there, to another one. They were the only creatures moving on it. Chico's nerves started to twang. From the safety of the corral, the openness felt perfect. Being out here made him feel exposed, unsheltered.

At last, they turned back toward the ranch buildings, as small as square hay bales in the distance. Good. Chico was ready to be done with straight lines.

But four Beasts had crowded close to the fence behind them, cutting them off from home. The sticks on their heads gleamed in the sun, wickedly pointed. There were fences on both sides. There was no way around . . .

Behind his swiveling ears, Sierra said, "Uh, Mom?"

"Don't look at them, Sierra!" It was the calm voice Sierra's mother used when she gave Chico a shot, telling him he wouldn't feel a thing. "If you look, he'll look. Just watch my back. We'll show him it's okay."

Chico knew "it's okay." People used those words when something alarming was happening, and they wanted to pretend that it wasn't. The queen walked steadily on, ever closer to the Beasts. Chico's heart raced, and his feet slowed. He felt Sierra reach for the saddle horn, which only deepened his fear. He must be good. He must be brave. But what if he couldn't? What if he simply had to run? He sent a whinny after the queen. *You sure about this?*

She ignored him. No, not *ignore,* exactly. Her tail flirted sassily. Her hips swayed. She arched her neck and pricked her ears. *Look at me!* her body said. *Just look!* The Beasts huddled at her approach. Their breath whooshed. A tail lifted–*splat-splat-splat-splat.* Then they turned, blundering into each other, and trotted away from the road.

Startled, Chico stopped in his tracks. *Wow! She just totally backed them off!*

Now the queen was getting ahead of him. If the Beasts were afraid of her, Chico's place was by her side. She could protect him. He jogged to catch up, and she slashed her tail at him. *Stay back! Who's queen?*

You. You rule!

"See?" Mom said to Chico. "That didn't kill you." That was her *after*-sting voice. Chico wished she'd give him a carrot like she did after the needle. He could really use a carrot right now.

The next day they took the same ride. The Beasts kept their distance.

Then the following morning, Sierra and Addie, carrying backpacks, walked down the road and got onto a school bus. In the afternoon, the bus came back, winding across the distant hills. The dog ran down the ranch road in a self-important way, and after a while, reappeared with the girls. Addie's chatter reached Chico long before they came into sight.

"Hey, wouldn't it be great if we could train the horses to come meet us? Then we wouldn't have to walk."

Sierra didn't answer. A glum, worried feeling radiated from her. Chico remembered how thrilled she'd seemed when they first met. Would she ever be like that again?

The girls went into the house, came out wearing jeans and boots, and put saddles on the horses. Down the ranch road; back again. Addie talked and talked. Sierra didn't say much. The Beasts stayed far away.

The next day, the same ride. The day after, again. And he used to think circles were boring!

On the fourth day, a single Beast was at the fence when they headed out. The earlier rides had been so dull that Chico was almost pleased to see it, fearsome though it seemed. He felt Sierra grab the saddle horn, but Addie gabbled on, and the queen just jogged straight toward it.

Would this Beast run? It wasn't moving. What if it didn't? What if it attacked? All Chico's muscles went hard. He could feel how his rough trot bounced Sierra, but he couldn't help it. If he could just hold it together, if he could just scoot past the creature–

The Beast ducked its head and lunged out of the way.

Thank goodness! Why couldn't it have done that right away? Chico put his ears back at the retreating hulk. If the fence wasn't there, he'd thunder after it, give it a good scare.

"Hey, Chico, what are you thinking about?" Sierra's voice had a hint of that light, bright, sparkly sound from the first day. "You want to chase that cow, don't you? I wonder if Mom could be right!"

Two days later, the bus didn't come, and the girls saddled up right after breakfast. Mom came over to talk to them.

"I'm glad Chico's bored with the road," she said. "That was the whole idea, to get him comfortable with his new surroundings. So I'm fine with you riding in the pasture, as long as you steer clear of cows."

"Chico's getting braver," Sierra said.

Mom said, "I'm trusting you to look after your sister, Sierra. Ride slowly and take it easy around the cattle."

"We'll take it easy," Sierra replied. The girls rode out through the pasture gate. The broad meadow spread before them, inviting Chico's legs to run.

"You don't need to take care of me," Addie said. "I'm a good rider."

"I know," Sierra said. "But Mom's watching."

Addie looked back. "I don't see her."

"Even if you don't see her, she's watching! And Dad is even worse!"

Talk talk talk. Chico snatched at the bit. Sierra let him jog, then lifted into a gentle lope. The queen kept pace. They headed toward the line where grass met sky. Gradually, another rolling swathe of grass appeared behind it, rimmed by rocky mountains. Beasts looked up as they passed.

Finally, Sierra swung Chico around to face the way they'd come. He saw only horizon. The ranch buildings were completely cut off from view. Chico couldn't even smell home; the wind was blowing from the wrong direction.

Sierra took a deep breath. "Addie, I want to try something. I have to find out. Do you *promise* not to tell Mom?"

Addie didn't answer, but she did stop chattering.

A small group of Beasts grazed nearby; four of them side by side. Sierra turned Chico toward them and asked him to walk.

His heart thudded. They outnumbered him! What was she thinking?

He felt the rein on his neck, turning him slightly to one side; zig.

Rein on the other side; zag.

Zig, zag, zig, zag; very slowly Sierra was riding him closer, and still closer. There came a moment when all four Beasts stopped grazing and bunched together, staring at him, pointing their paddle-shaped ears. Their breathing sounded deep and emotional.

Chico braced and stared back. Sierra put her hand on his neck reassuringly. Beasts didn't seem to make her nervous, but what did she know? She wasn't even an adult. Could he trust her?

Her legs squeezed his sides. Another step forward? *No way!* What if he couldn't be good anymore? What if he had to run, duck out from under her, and just bolt for the horizon? She could be hurt, and she was small. Young.

Bossy. Her legs squeezed again, and without meaning to, Chico took a step. Sierra squeezed again. Another. One more and he was going to blow!

The Beasts flapped their ears, tossed their heads.

Then they all turned toward each other, each trying to get into the middle of the group. There was no middle left, and they walked away.

Chico stopped in disbelief. *Away?* They were walking *away*? He felt suddenly larger, filled with energy. He snatched for more rein. Make 'em go faster!

Sierra gave a high-pitched yip of delight and turned him away from the retreating Beasts. "*Yes!* You like that, Chico, don't you? Good boy!"

"You moved them just the way Dad does," Addie said. "Only he walks."

"We didn't chase them!" Sierra said quickly.

"I know!" Addie said. "Dad hates anything chasing his cows. Chico looks proud." She hesitated. "So–do you like him now?"

Sierra reached down and hugged Chico's neck. "I like him a *lot*! That was the problem. I was worried he wouldn't be able to do cutting, but–wow!" She sat up straight in the saddle again, laughing. Everything about her felt light and breezy again, like when Chico first met her.

They turned back toward home, both girls chattering. Chico matched his steps to the queen's, eyeing the groups of Beasts they passed. Now he saw them in a whole new way. They could be chased! Big as they were, they were afraid of *him*!

Chico knew all about power. The horse that can make another horse move out of the way is the boss. He could do that with his brothers, even though he was the youngest;

never with his mother or sister, certainly not with the queen. But he'd just moved four Beasts at once! Could he move *every* Beast?

They came over the big rise and a large cluster of Beasts were right in front of them. *Let's get them,* he suggested, dancing, bobbing his head, and pricking his ears at the creatures.

Sierra laughed and patted him on the shoulder. "Sorry, hotshot! We're in sight of the house." Instead of moving toward the animals, she swung Chico toward the edge of the woods, letting him lope to vent his feelings, outdistancing Addie and the queen.

A strong Beast-scent emanated from the trees. Chico sensed movement. A second later, the woods erupted in a crash of brush and cracking branches. Chico whirled as a great black Beast emerged from the pines, head lowered, charging straight at the queen.

CHAPTER 4

THE QUEEN SHIED. ADDIE SHRIEKED.

Chico felt the reins on his neck and Sierra's smooth boot heels driving into his sides, jumping him back there, toward the charging Beast.

He leaped without thinking. He didn't need to think. *His* queen. *His* human! They were part of his new herd, and just as he'd once charged the pit bull back at Dean's, and just as he'd faced down a blowing, crinkling monster–which had turned out to be an empty trash bag, but no one had known that at the time–he flung himself between his herd and the threat. That's what young male horses were for; to fight, sometimes to die, for the herd.

The Beast stopped in its tracks, blinking. Chico stopped, too, facing it down. It was uncertain, he realized. It was of two minds. How did he know that? He didn't know how–he just did. He took a fast step forward, ears laced back in a menacing expression.

The animal gave an uneasy moan and turned, trotting back toward the woods. Chico lunged after it, jaws wide.

His teeth closed sharply on the boney base of its tail. Sierra's surprised shriek was dim in his ears. He leaned on the reins, biting again, urging the beast ahead of him into a lumbering gallop. They crashed into the woods, and a small shape staggered upright from a bed of ferns, bleating. The Beast moaned again, in a different tone of voice, and rushed to it.

Now Chico felt legs and reins and bit again, all urging him to turn, get out of the woods quickly. He loped back into the open, back to the queen. She stood with head high and ears flat, the picture of offended dignity. On her back, Addie clung to the saddle horn with her mouth hanging open.

Chico's whole body tingled. He felt twice his normal size. *Amazing! It ran away! Actually ran!* If Sierra hadn't stopped him, he could have chased it farther, much farther. He gazed across the pasture at the others. Beasts? No more. They were only cows. He could chase any of them, all of them, and he would again, the moment he got the chance.

Why hadn't he known about this before? Why had he wasted his life chasing stray dogs and garbage bags? All along, cows had existed, and he was born to chase them.

Sierra stroked Chico's neck again and again. "Chico, you were wonderful!"

Addie said, "You guys looked just like Misty Lassiter on one of her horses!"

Sierra heard a sound and looked toward the ranch house. Far off, the four-wheeler came bounding over the grass toward them. Dad's hat lay back on the grass, and the dog was even farther back, chasing the vehicle intently and silently.

"How does he *do* that?" Sierra asked. "Remember, Addie–you can't get away with *anything* on this ranch. Dad sees *everything*!"

Dad slowed down when he was still a good distance away, so as not to frighten the horses. Chico stood rock still, completely unconcerned. Sierra's heart swelled with love. He was so steady, so cheerful. A perfect horse . . .

"You girls all right?" Dad asked. "I was just coming out of the barn, and I saw what happened."

"The cow has a calf in the pines," Sierra said. "It looked pretty new."

"I wonder which critter it is. I don't mind a cow being a little aggressive about a new calf–that'll save it from coyotes. But if she's going to make a habit of charging people, we can't have that."

"She charged me and Queenie," Addie said. "But Sierra and Chico chased her away."

"I saw that, too," Dad said. He reached up, felt for his

hat, and, not finding it, rumpled his flattened hair. "Your mother thought he'd come around."

Sierra felt her face turn red, but she didn't say anything.

"I'm no horseman," Dad went on, "but I remember Pop telling me how they used to start colts when he was cowboying. They'd ride them at the drag end of a trail herd, so every cow they saw was moving away from them. By the time they got wherever they were going, there wasn't a cow those horses wouldn't chase. I'm bringing some stock in for Misty tomorrow. Maybe you girls could ride along behind?"

Sierra nodded.

Dad smiled at her. "Stars in your eyes again, kid. It's good to see!"

Sierra rode home, considering the strangeness of getting horse advice from Dad. He was firmly attached to his four-wheeler, his dog, and his own ways of moving cattle; mostly on foot, using the slow zigzags to gather the cows in and nudge them in the direction he wanted. Dad read books about it, and with his methods, he could do almost everything he needed–except bring stock in from the mountain pastures. Mom used to do that on Scout, and last fall when Scout was too old, Dad borrowed a cowboy from another ranch.

But though other ranchers raised their eyebrows and sometimes laughed at him, Dad was as good a cowman as any of them. His father and grandfather were ranchers, too, and to Sierra, this felt like a bit of horse wisdom passed down from them. Ride a young horse behind a herd. Let him watch cows going away from him. It made a lot of sense. *Thank you, Dad!* Thank you, Grampy.

. . .

THE NEXT AFTERNOON, THE HORSES FOLLOWED the four-wheeler to the high pasture. It stretched halfway up the mountainside. Large gray rocks loomed up out of the grass like lurking predators. The cattle up here were smaller, with only nubs of horns. They were more skittish, too, bunching in alarm at the sight of the horses.

"Stay back," Dad told the girls. He poured the contents of a couple of buckets of feed onto the ground, and backed the four-wheeler out of the way. Chico smelled grain and sweet molasses. The dog whined. Dad put a hand on his collar, and he hushed.

The young cattle crowded and jostled around the grain. Dad edged the four-wheeler closer. He released the dog, pointing him to a parallel spot on the other side of the bunch. He pointed to Addie and Sierra, too, showing them where he wanted them to go. Every move was slow and quiet, and the cattle didn't raise their heads.

When the cattle finished eating and began to look around, Dad gently moved the four-wheeler even closer. On the other side, the dog crept forward on his belly. The queen took a step, too.

So slow! Chico couldn't stand it. He danced, jigged, sidled, snatching at the bit, pushing his head low, throwing it high in the air. *Come on! Let's move these babies!* The cattle turned their ears toward him nervously, and Dad said, "Keep him farther back, Sierra."

"I'm trying."

The reins were tight now. The bit felt hard and strong in Chico's mouth. But he could ignore that. He was much stronger than Sierra, and he knew what he wanted–

She did something with one rein. Chico found himself facing the wrong direction. How did she do that? He whirled after the cows–and there he was, facing the wrong way again.

He put his head down, leaned hard on the bit, and charged after the slow-moving herd.

Ow! She did it again, and this time it stung. It looked like he'd have to do what she wanted.

But he didn't have to make it easy! Chico shook his head, even hitched up his back end and threatened to buck. He'd never been this bad before, ever, even in the earliest days when Dean was teaching him to be ridden. But he'd never wanted to do anything as much as he wanted to chase those cows.

Dad looked back in concern. The queen flattened her ears and swung her head at Chico, showing her strong yellow teeth.

The four-wheeler dropped back. Dad said, "This isn't working. Take him home, Sierra, okay?"

Sierra turned Chico around and pushed him into a lope–away from the cows. *What was she? An idiot?* Chico thought. Sierra headed him down a trail among the tall dark pines. He listened to the herd moving above him on the mountainside, glimpsed them through the jack pines, then left them behind as he picked his way down the foothills, bright with mountain flowers, fragrant with sage brush. A cool dry wind bent the grass stems. The wide sky curved above. It was the vastness he'd sensed and craved in his cramped paddock at Dean's, and now Chico had to leave that openness–and the cows–behind.

It was so unfair!

Back in the horse corral, Sierra said, "You're all lathered up, silly!"

She got a bucket of warm water and washed Chico's back and chest and belly. He stamped at the droplets that tickled his legs like flies. He flattened his ears when Sierra sponged his face. He'd never felt this frustrated in his whole life! At last he'd found the thing he truly wanted to do, and this girl wouldn't let him do it.

The cattle trailed off the mountain in a long, slow-moving line, and they finally reached the corral next to his. Addie and the queen drove them through the gate at a snail's pace.

Sierra turned Chico loose. He rolled in the dirt, until he was crusty and coated, stood up and shook himself, and trotted to the fence. He put his head over the top rail. The cattle retreated to the far side of the corral.

Chico stepped back to get a bite of hay. The cattle relaxed. One or two took a step toward him. It was as if he had been pressing on them somehow, and now they had a tiny bit more space.

He took another few steps back. More cattle drifted in his direction.

Chico stood with his head down, watching them. He was perfectly quiet. The cattle seemed to forget him. They explored their new surroundings. When one neared the fence, Chico stepped decisively toward it.

The cow shied to the left. Chico pounced in that direction, mirroring the cow's move. She gave him a bug-eyed stare and trotted back to the group. Chico took up his stance again, waiting until another cow approached the fence.

What a great game!

He didn't spare much attention for the people watching from the porch, but after a few minutes Sierra came to the corral with an apple and Chico's halter.

"You're sleeping in the barn tonight," she told him. "Dad doesn't want you bugging his cows–but you're really starting to act like a cutting horse!"

Interfering again. But the apple was good, as always, and he was tired.

After breakfast the next day, Chico was allowed back in the horse corral. The young cows had done all their exploring. They clustered at their hay rack with their backs to Chico, then lay at the far end of the pen and chewed their cuds at him. The constant grinding of their jaws, the pause and gentle belch as the cud came up, was all fascinating. These animals *belonged* to him. He was born to manage them, boss them, take care of them, and though he longed to gallop into their corral and scatter them in all directions, too, Chico also felt profoundly content to just be near them.

That afternoon, just after Sierra and Addie got home from school, a truck and stock trailer came along the dusty road. It was the first strange vehicle Chico had seen since he came here. A young woman got out. She was slim, straight, hatted, and booted. Testing the air, Chico caught a scent from her: horses and dust and some kind of flowers.

Dad came out of the barn, and they talked. People always talked so much! All the faces kept turning toward him, and the group drifted toward the horse corral. The queen bustled to the fence and thrust her head between the rails, with a warning swish of her tail at Chico. *Who's queen?*

The young woman patted the queen and climbed up on the rail to look at Chico. "That is a *nice* quarter horse! How long have you had him?"

"A couple of weeks."

"How come I haven't heard about it? Is he your cutting-horse prospect?"

Sierra hesitated. "He's supposed to be, but he was afraid of cows–"

"Not a problem. A lot of real cowy horses are scared of the first cow they see."

"Oh," Sierra said. "Anyway, he's over that. Now he wants to chase them all the time."

"That's worse, actually, but we can deal with it. Tell me about him."

Sierra talked. The young woman listened, with her eyes focused on Chico. She gave him a funny feeling, confident and edgy at the same time–like nothing he could do would surprise her, but that she might surprise *him.* He drifted closer to Sierra. She'd surprised him a few times too, especially yesterday, but he knew she was on his side.

Sierra could tell that Misty liked Chico. But something was bothering the trainer. Sierra could tell that, too, especially when Misty deliberately changed the subject and started talking about the cattle with Dad.

Misty leased young stock from him to train her cutting horses with. That was a stretch for Dad, who believed in a stress-free life for cattle. But he also believed in caring for his land, and grazing some yearlings at Misty's preserved his own grass and soil. So far the heifers were thriving, and the extra money helped. Ranching was a hard way to make a living.

Mom came home, and everyone settled down on the porch; drinks, chips, feet up on the rail. "I love when you come over," Mom said to Misty. "I practically never sit on my own porch like this."

"I never sit on my porch either," Misty said. "It's a strange life, being a horse trainer."

"Try being a large-animal veterinarian!" Mom said.

The adults talked about this, that, the other. How important the cattle were to Misty: "Because it's weird, you know? This sport is getting huge, and at the same time, there's fewer and fewer cattle ranches in this country. It starts to feel artificial sometimes."

The talk finally circled back to Chico, and Misty put her soda can down.

"I blame myself," she said.

Sierra's heart did a double-thump. *Here it comes!*

"When I said I'd help Sierra get into cutting, I was assuming you'd find a horse that had some cutting experience. Novice teaching novice isn't a good combination."

"But he's so well trained," Mom said quickly, coming to Chico's defense. "For reining, not cutting, but I thought that would be a good foundation."

"Maybe," Misty said. "Anyway, my fault. If I wasn't so crazy busy, I'd have helped you find the right horse. And now you've got this guy–and he's such a perfect quarter horse, Sierra! I'd want to give him a good solid try if I were you. What about you?" She turned to Mom. "Are you thinking about another horse?"

Mom shook her head. "Not ready yet. I got Scout when I was Sierra's age. You don't–" She cleared her throat. "You don't replace a horse like that easily."

Sierra swallowed at the lump in her own throat, staring down at the corral. Chico stood, head down, facing the young cattle. The sun gleamed on his honey-colored coat. Dark dapples were starting to show as he shed his winter hair. As if he sensed her looking at him, he turned, and his lightning-streak blaze flashed at her like a friendly wave.

Sierra lifted her fingers to wave back, but he was already looking at the heifers again.

Misty was watching, too.

"That horse has a *lot* of cow. What the heck! Let's break the rules! I'll train both of you, separately. Then I'll put you together and we'll see what we've got."

CHAPTER 5

CHICO CLIMBED EAGERLY INTO MISTY'S stock trailer, lured by the thrilling scent of cattle. The ride was short, though. He'd barely started to eat from the hay net when the trailer slowed and stopped, and he stepped out into another new world.

Same huge sky, mountain backdrop, sweep of high dry grassland. There was even a small log ranch house. But everything else was completely different.

There was a big metal barn and a broad, covered arena nearby. Dust rose from a high-walled pen across the yard, and Chico heard cows moving. From another pen came a creaking sound, like the clothesline next door at Dean's house, where the neighbor used to reel out her sheets on sunny mornings. Chico thought he heard a horse moving in that pen.

A pickup truck drove out. Another drove in. Five more were parked in the sun. Everywhere, young people in big hats rode horses between the buildings, or clustered at the backs of trucks, talking. They all seemed calm, purposeful, cheerful.

"Hi, there!" Misty rode toward them on a superior-looking palomino mare. The mare didn't need to say *Queen!* She just flicked a slender ear at Chico, and he suddenly felt meek and polite.

"Take Chico into the barn and saddle up," Misty said to Sierra. "I've got a lesson to finish, and then we'll see what we've got here."

Sierra led Chico into the barn. It was big and full of horses. She tied him in the aisle, and then went back to the family truck for brushes, bridle, and saddle. Sierra was nervous. Chico felt her hands shake as she groomed and saddled him.

After a while, Dad said, "Looks like they're done." Sierra unhitched Chico and led him out. A sweating horse was led from the high-sided corral. Misty, on the palomino, waved.

"Bring him over." She dismounted, and Sierra put Chico's reins in Misty's hand. Chico tried to watch everything at once–Sierra, the new mare, Misty–while still listening for and smelling cattle. Where *were* they?

Misty and Sierra talked–but who could listen to people with all this going on? Then Misty swung up onto his back, and Chico had to give her all his attention. Unlike Dean or Sierra, Misty seemed to sink down through the saddle and become part of him. That could be good or bad. Chico didn't know which yet, only that without seeming to touch the reins or use her legs, she was moving him into the high-walled pen. She was good!

The weathered plywood walls blocked his view. The footing was sandy, not too deep; good. Somewhere beyond the plywood, cattle lurked. Chico traveled around the pen with one ear tilted toward the wall, listening for them. Misty asked him to pick up the pace: jog, then lope; some circles, a few spins, and sliding stops. Chico didn't hold out on her; something told him that wouldn't be wise. He didn't try any shortcuts, either.

Misty reined him to a stop at one end of the arena, touched something on her waist, and her voice came from the speaker-boxes as well as from up there in the saddle. "All right, Joe."

A section of wall opened. Chico raised his head, watching intently as two young heifers trotted through, ears back and tails anxiously high. *Yes!* He'd known there were cattle! *His* cattle, the same lively, wiggly yearlings he'd helped bring in the other day. It would be fun to make them run–

Misty's soft, clever hand suddenly seemed made of iron, unbudgeable. It allowed him forward only slowly, only a little. Closer, closer–the young cattle started to move away from him and the iron hand froze, keeping him at exactly that distance. The heifers walked around the outside wall. Chico pranced beside them, level with the last cow's hip. Once, twice around the pen–

The hand relaxed. Chico spurted forward. The cattle swung around and went back the other way. Chico would have darted after them, but the hand prevented that.

Misty said, "Joe, let the rest of them in."

The gate swung wide and fifteen more young cattle came through. They milled around, close to each other, watching everything suspiciously. When most of them finally stood still, Misty's hand relented. Chico danced toward them, with low, purring snorts. *Oh boy! This is going to be good!*

"You weren't exaggerating," Misty's loudspeaker voice called out to Sierra. "This is getting a little Western!"

Closer. Closer. Misty was aiming Chico straight toward the cows. But she expected him to go *slow*? To heck with that! Chico tucked his chin, the reins flapped loose for a second, and he bounced into the middle of the herd.

With startled bawls, the cattle scattered in all directions. Which to chase? Chico hesitated, and Misty caught up with his mouth again–not harshly, but he felt her anger. *Yikes!* He'd just displeased a *real* queen.

Dad didn't say anything. He didn't need to. Sierra saw him press his lips shut and take a deep breath, and her face went hot with embarrassment. Chico was being *awful.* She didn't dare look up as Misty rode close.

But if Misty was angry, she concealed it well. "Mr. Bonteen, that wasn't cutting," she said. "We *never* harass your cows like that. Sierra, hop up on Ladybird and let's see what you can do."

Ladybird? The famous Ladybird? The one in Sierra's Misty pictures? Ladybird was quarter horse royalty. More important, she was a world-class cutting horse; umpteen championships, a gazillion dollars in earnings . . . Oh sure, just climb on! What if Sierra did something wrong? What if–

She got herself in the saddle somehow and looked half blindly toward Misty, who shouted, *"Smile!"*

Sierra jumped and almost fell off Ladybird. Misty's chuckle filled the ring.

"Seriously. Relax. Ride in a circle down there and let me watch you."

Sierra obeyed. She felt stiff, and she knew that was wrong–but what could she do about it?

"Slouch in the saddle," Misty instructed. "Make your back soft and curved, just like a banana. Try to sit on the back pockets of your jeans."

I know that, Sierra thought. *At least, I've read it . . .*

She let her spine soften, felt her way onto her back pockets.

"Good!" Misty said. "Now mash down in the stirrups, point your toes out–good. That's the cutter's slouch. It'd win you last prize in an equitation class, but that's what keeps you on a cutting horse."

She had Sierra jog, then lope.

"Now, grab the horn with your right hand and push on it. Feel how that gets you deeper in the saddle? That's what'll really save your butt."

While Sierra practiced, Misty and Chico gathered the cows in a bunch. Chico danced up and down. Foam flecked his jaw and spattered his chest. He was acting like a raving maniac, not a well-mannered town boy. Somehow Misty kept him under control while seeming to ignore his bad behavior, but–

"Now"–the microphone picked up Chico's loud breathing as well as Misty's voice–"ride Ladybird right into the bunch, at a walk. Wander through, pick a cow–any cow, as long as it's near the edge–and just stare at it. And see what happens."

This was it! Holding her rein hand high, Sierra rode into the bunched cattle. It was like gliding a boat into deep water. The animals swirled and eddied around her, their backs just below the level of her knees. Ladybird moved so gently, the cows were barely disturbed. Sierra noticed the one with scars from an earlier coyote attack.

"Pick one," Misty reminded her.

Sierra focused on Scar. Without any more telling than that, Ladybird also focused. With slight movements left, right, left, the mare guided the heifer toward the outside edge of the herd, and then beyond it–

"Drop your hand!" Misty barked.

Oh yeah. The rider chose, but the horse delivered. Once you committed to your cow and got it outside the herd, you were supposed to turn things over to the horse. Sierra rested her left hand on Ladybird's neck and braced her right against the horn.

Suddenly, the heifer realized she was out there alone, away from all the others. She ducked back toward them and *wham!* Ladybird spun into her path, crouching low. Sierra gasped. A cutting horse dropping on a cow felt like a fast ride on a down elevator.

"Stay loose! Mash down in your stirrups–"

The heifer dodged right, Ladybird followed, and Sierra's liver and a few other internal organs slammed into her rib cage. She pushed back on the saddle horn, which snugged her down in the saddle. She felt like a passenger–better hang on tight, or she'd be an ex-passenger!

With a moan, the heifer made a run for it. She wanted to get past the horse and dodge back into the group. Swift as a pouncing cat, Ladybird shadowed her and brought her to a halt. They went nose to nose, locked in a trance-like stare–

"And quit," Misty said. "Pick up the reins and give her a pat on the neck."

In a daze, Sierra obeyed. She'd just cut her first cow. She'd brought it to a standstill. She felt scattered, as if she were in three places at once. It was *hard,* trying to focus on her own body, on the horse beneath her, and on the cow. Misty made it look so easy and full of grace–

Misty rode toward Dad, motioning Sierra to follow her. She got off Chico, and Sierra slid off Ladybird.

"Okay," Misty said. "Here's what *ought* to happen. Sierra learns on a horse that's already good at competition cutting. Chico gets started right by a good trainer. In a couple of years, you two get together and burn up the youth circuit, because you've both got buckets of talent."

A couple of years? Sierra thought. She looked at the ground.

"The thing is," Misty went on, "is that Chico's cow crazy, and he's learned to ignore a rider. But he's the horse you have, and he probably fell into your lap for a reason. So leave him here with me for a few weeks. I'll work him, you'll do some work on Ladybird, and then we'll see if he'll partner up with you. If he does, he might make a cutting horse. But he's got to learn that a rider is a partner, not an adversary. If he doesn't–" Misty stopped herself. "But we're going to teach him that, so I won't finish that sentence. Unsaddle him and put him in the fourth stall on the right, Sierra. And I'll see you tomorrow afternoon."

CHAPTER 6

CHICO'S NEW STALL AT MISTY'S PLACE HAD A paddock where he could graze and play nipping games with neighbors in other paddocks. But when the afternoon wind blew off the mountains, he thought he could smell the ranch. He missed it.

In the morning, people fed the horses, cleaned the stalls, and pickup trucks started arriving. Later Joe, the barn manager, led Chico out, brushed and saddled him, and Misty appeared.

Misty meant cattle; good. But she was awfully bossy. With mixed feelings, Chico followed her toward the small pen, the one that had squeaked. She opened the gate and led him inside.

The pen was empty. Chico looked along the high wall. If this was like yesterday, one of those panels would open and cattle would come in. Only he didn't sense cattle that close this time.

Misty warmed him up: walk, jog, lope, circles. Backup. Lots of backup. Then she turned him to face the center of the pen, and she did something with the saddle horn. Chico felt her push lightly, and there was a tiny clicking sound. Out in the middle of the empty space, something moved.

Chico threw up his head and stared. *Danger? Run?* It was some kind of bird, maybe, swooping across at chest level . . . no, it looked more like laundry being reeled out on a clothesline, only much faster.

Abruptly, it stopped.

Chico tested the air with flared nostrils. It wasn't alive, he decided, in spite of the way it moved. It *was* laundry–cloth, anyway–and it had been outdoors a long time. It didn't have the soapy wet smell he associated with laundry, and there was only one piece, light colored, with a dark shape on it that looked like a cow's head–

It snapped back in the other direction.

And into the middle again.

And back again.

Chico put his head down with a sigh and sniffed the ground, hoping for the scent of cattle. But there had been no cows here lately, only horses. His ears tipped out to the sides.

"Am I boring you, kid?" Misty said. "Let's fix that."

She touched the horn again. Chico heard the click, and with a thin clothesline squeak, the cloth snapped into motion. Misty clapped her legs against his sides. He leaped forward, following the moving laundry.

"Good," Misty said.

Good? She *wanted* him to chase it? He thundered after the small cloth, easily catching up.

Suddenly, the laundry stopped. So did Chico; not because he wanted to, but because of the way Misty sat in the saddle. It wasn't the way Dean had stopped him. Her hand on the reins pulled back, not up, and Chico's head stayed low, which Dean would not have liked.

Dean would want a rollback now, a swift turn on the haunches. Anticipating, Chico tried that, felt a firm leg holding him still–and then the laundry took off again, back across the pen, and Misty spun him after it.

Left. Stop.

Right. Stop.

After a few repetitions, it started to feel like a game.

More repetitions. It wasn't a very *good* game. Chico was supposed to pounce after the laundry, race in a line parallel to it, never getting close; stop when it stopped, and wait for its next move. He never got to win, to go up to the laundry and pull it off the line. He'd done that once, when Dean's fence broke and all the horses got loose in the neighborhood. He had pulled several pieces of cloth down from a line and trampled them with his front hooves,

and somebody in a house screamed. It was f
snatch at the bit, with his pointing ears, Chi
that game to Misty. She ignored him.

Why weren't people more creative? All right already! He had the concept. But Misty wanted more from him. Chico couldn't figure out what, and he didn't much care. This was as boring as circles.

Misty stopped him and patted his neck. "Good enough for your first lesson."

First lesson? There was going to be *more* of this?

. . .

FOR SIERRA, THE NEXT THREE WEEKS PASSED IN a blur: school, ride the bus to Misty's place; change her clothes, say hi to Chico, saddle Ladybird and hurry to the arena for her lesson. She worked with flags mostly, learning to sit right and stay with Ladybird's explosive bursts of speed.

Helping Sierra saddle one afternoon at the end of the third week, Misty explained again why she used the flag so much. "It lets you practice a move over and over. A cow never makes the same move twice. And the Bird never gets bored with it, not like some horses. Girl's got a work ethic!" She patted the mare's neck, and Ladybird turned her head into the crook of Misty's arm.

Ladybird never does anything like that with me, Sierra

thought. Riding a horse that loved somebody else was a good way to feel invisible.

"How does Chico like the flag?" she asked. With school, she hadn't been able to get there in time to watch any of his lessons.

Misty shrugged. "He's superfast and athletic, but he's probably a little bored."

Sierra opened her mouth, and closed it. She was just a kid, a newbie, and this was Misty Lassiter. But Chico didn't handle boredom well. That was why he'd soured as a reining horse. She had to say it. "He's really *interested* in cows."

"Yes," Misty said dryly. "And things still get real Western when he's around them!"

Sierra felt herself flush. She knew that "Western" wasn't something a cutting horse should be around cows.

"But forget Chico right now," Misty added quickly. "This afternoon we're simulating a cutting competition. Bring the Bird along." She mounted another horse and rode toward the covered arena. Three other students waited outside. Sierra hadn't gotten to know any of them yet, and she forgot the girls' names the minute they were introduced, but she remembered the name of the tall boy, Randall.

Misty backed her horse around to face the students.

"Lecture time. Cutting is the only sport I know where you ask four of your biggest rivals to help you out in your performance, and where you ride your heart out for somebody you're competing against. When I talk about things getting 'Western,' I don't often mean it as a compliment. But this is Western in the best sense—the cowboy ethic of friendly, good sportsmanship. So, in this lesson, focus on being good help, as well as having a good run."

Sierra thought of her cutting posters, and the countless video clips she'd watched. Each showed one horse, one rider, one cow, dueling it out together. In reality you needed your team—a team of rivals.

Misty said, "At a show, you'll ask four people to be your help during your run. I've hired your help for you today. Sierra, you're up first, Randall and I will be your turn-back riders, and the girls will be herd holders. Then we'll rotate." She nodded to Joe, who opened the door and let them into the arena.

The herd holders rode down to the far end; Joe opened another gate to let the cattle in, and one of the herd holders settled them, riding back and forth in front of the cows to teach them to stay near the back wall. Then that same holder tested them, walking her horse through the herd from back to front and side to side. So much of cutting happened at a walk—again, not like the pictures.

The settler rode to her station at the side of the herd; now she was the second herd holder. Sierra looked at

Misty, who nodded for her to go ahead. "Remember, your time starts when you pass the yellow stripe on the wall. You've got two and a half minutes." She and Randall positioned themselves near the center of the arena, and Sierra rode forward.

She walked Ladybird past the yellow stripe and into the herd from the right. The cattle crowded each other, each heifer trying to be the one in the middle, but none panicked. The mare moved among them as intent as a stalking heron, ears pricked, noticing each cow in turn.

Misty said, "Two and a half minutes goes by fast!"

No time to think. Holding her rein-hand chest high, Sierra turned Ladybird toward the front of the herd. She was supposed to be making her deep cut, bringing one animal out from well inside the herd, but it seemed like she had most of the cows in front of her, all walking and shoving and jostling toward the turn-back riders.

The cows on the edges of the group turned back toward the main herd. Casually. They weren't too worried. There were three left out in the open, two Herefords and a black baldy. The baldy looked like a nice cow; bright-eyed, alert, but not hocky. She'd make a game of it, an intelligent try to get back into the herd, not stand there dumbly, or hightail it for the hills. *There's an advantage to being a ranch girl,* Sierra thought. *I do know cows.*

She rode Ladybird toward the three, still at the same slow walk. One Hereford cocked its tail and started pooping. The other Hereford and the baldy ambled back toward the bunch. Sierra started to rein Ladybird after the cow of her choice.

"No time, Ranch Girl!" Misty called. "Poopy Pants is yours. Look happy with the cow you've got."

Cutting was showmanship. No matter what happened, you tried to look like you did it on purpose. Smoothing out her expression, Sierra advanced another step toward the pooping heifer, framed her between Ladybird's ears, and dropped her hand.

The cow's head swiveled around and a horrified look came over her. *OMG! I'm out here all alone!* She made a run to the left, and Ladybird exploded into action, so fast her mane lifted from her neck in a white cloud. Sierra's whole body jolted. She felt her hat fly off.

Ladybird raced parallel with the heifer. The heifer stopped, Ladybird stopped, and Sierra shoved back on the horn, settling herself deeper in the saddle. She curved her back, sank her weight down into the stirrups, and stared hard at the cow. She was ready now. The cow dashed right; Ladybird was on her. Wind whipped Sierra's shirt and hair, but her body stayed supple and in sync with the horse.

The heifer stopped and turned toward the far wall, saw

the turn-back riders, and kept twirling, all the way around in a circle to face Ladybird. And twirled again. Sierra could almost hear her thinking: *What should I do? What should I do?* The cow made a dash at Misty, who rode toward her, slapping her thigh. The sharp sound turned the cow back to Sierra, and they dueled again, short dodges back and forth, until the cow turned and trotted away with her head up.

"And quit," Misty reminded.

Sierra came back to reality with a start. For those few seconds, her whole brain had been taken up with that one cow. She patted Ladybird's neck, lifted the reins, and backed her up a few steps, while the heifer they'd been working trotted around the outside of the arena and merged back into the herd.

Sierra needed to cut two more cows. She rode into the herd again, peeled off a small group from the outside edge, and moved them toward the middle of the arena. Toward her fallen hat.

A black heifer stopped to sniff the hat, legs braced, ears stiff with shock at seeing the strange object there. Sierra felt her temper rise. Why did this stupid cow have to call attention to her bad riding? You'll pay for that, Blackie! She edged the heifer away from the group, worked her, let her back in the herd, and cut another cow. Just as she committed, the finishing buzzer went off. Wow. Two and a half minutes wasn't much time, but it could feel like forever.

Ladybird dropped to a walk. The herd holders left the cows and ambled forward with Sierra, the turn-back riders met them and reversed direction, and they all walked out of the arena in a group, the way they would at a real show. Someone else's turn now. In a few minutes, Sierra would be a herd holder.

The group of riders passed by her hat–amazingly, it hadn't been trampled–and Randall bent gracefully from the saddle, scooped it up, and handed it to her. He really was cute. Flushing, Sierra jammed the hat on her head. Granules of dirt trickled down her neck.

"A lot to like about that run," Misty said. "Sure, you lost your hat, but you could have fallen off. I've done that. You took your eye off the cow for a second, is all."

"Oh!" Sierra remembered looking down at Ladybird's mane.

"*Never* look down at the horse. Watch the cow. She's the one that knows where you're going next. You've gotta forget you even have a horse under you, or you won't."

"Yeah."

Misty went on. "There's a hundred details you need to learn for competition cutting–and we'll get to those!–but your instincts are great."

"But–," Sierra said. "I never did get the cow I wanted."

"Doesn't matter, as long as you make the judge think it's all going according to plan."

"Yeah, but–what if there was a cow I really *needed* to cut out? To give it a shot, or sell or something."

Misty laughed. "In that case, Ranch Girl, go for that baby! But that's real life. Competition cutting is a sport–the best in the world, in my opinion–but it's all make-believe."

Sierra nodded. She understood. *But I'd still rather get the cow I want,* she thought. She patted the mare's golden neck. Ladybird tipped one ear back at her, then pointed it straight ahead in her reserved and regal way. Sierra got the feeling Ladybird disapproved of riders who lost their hats.

"Can I ride Chico now?" Sierra asked. Chico liked her–she was pretty sure of that–and he didn't make her feel inferior. "I'm only a herd holder."

"There's no such thing as 'only a herd holder.' It's an important job," Misty said. She hesitated. "And I'm not sure he's ready. But . . . who's up next? Randall? All right with you if Sierra uses her bronco?"

Randall shrugged. "Don't see what harm it could do."

. . .

SIERRA! **CHICO CHORTLED DEEP IN HIS THROAT.** He missed her, living over here. Yes, he got ridden every day, but Misty didn't pamper him the way Sierra did. She didn't have the time.

Sierra didn't seem to have time today, either. She brushed him and saddled up quickly. She seemed agitated; now Chico started to feel that way himself.

Going into the covered arena, the quick change from sunshine to shadow half blinded Chico for a moment. He could sense cattle, dark shapes loosely grouped at the far end. Sierra headed him toward them, and for a moment panic flared along Chico's legs. *Beasts?*

His vision cleared. *Only cows.* He'd barely had a chance at cattle here; he danced slightly, and flicked his tail. *Let's–*

"No." Sierra walked him to one edge of the herd, turned him, made him stand. Another horse stood opposite, on the other side of the cattle. Three riders approached; the turn-back riders hung back, and the third, Randall, rode into the herd. The cattle stirred around his horse. Chico wanted to stir them, too, but Sierra wouldn't let him move. He pawed the dirt; a couple of nearby cows showed the whites of their eyes and mixed themselves deeper into the group. Misty shouted something, and Sierra backed Chico away from them.

Randall's horse was moving some cattle–slowly, at a walk, not the way Chico would have done it, but at least that horse was allowed to *do* something. Sierra let Chico move slightly forward now. They were helping Randall, but it could all go a whole lot faster–

Sierra turned her head to look at the herd. Chico felt her attention divide and weaken. The heifers paused between Randall and the turn-back riders, looking around, undecided. One swift move was all it would take–

Chico made the move! One lunge, and the heifers scattered in all directions. Chico took a gleeful bound after the nearest one, and Sierra caught him up short.

Randall turned angrily. "I can't believe–"

"Clock's ticking, Randall," Misty called. "Act like you are in charge, no matter what. Sierra, keep Chico back. *Wa-a-a-y* back."

Sierra turned him toward the herd. She was upset, Chico sensed. Well, so was he! All those cows got away! There was just one left. Randall and his horse went back and forth with it for a few seconds, then let it go. It trotted around the arena and dived back into the herd; Chico laid his ears back as it passed, but Sierra didn't let him take one step toward it.

Randall played with another cow, and then the buzzer went off, and they all turned from the herd. Sierra rode Chico forward, too. The rest of the horses walked, but Chico couldn't help prancing. All those cattle behind him, standing still. What a waste!

Randall turned to Sierra. To Chico, he sounded like Dean used to, when he was angry and trying to pretend he wasn't.

"I guess he really is a bronco! I thought Misty was joking."

Nobody else said anything until they were outside the arena. Then Misty beckoned to Sierra. "Ride over here with me. We need to talk."

CHAPTER 7

NUMBLY, SIERRA RODE AFTER MISTY. SHE'D just ruined Randall's run. She didn't know when she'd ever felt this miserable.

Randall was trying not to show his fury, because being a good sport was important in cutting. But it should never have happened. She should have stopped it.

In the driveway, out of earshot of anyone, Misty turned Ladybird around and looked soberly at Sierra. "It's time to face facts. Chico needs a *lot* of work–basic, kindergarten work, and this isn't the place for him to get it. If he was further along, I could have schooled him while I worked with other riders. But as he is now, he'd only interfere. These kids pay big bucks to come here. I've gotta give 'em their money's worth."

Sierra nodded. She couldn't speak.

"If you want to cut this year," Misty said in a gentler voice, "you can ride Ladybird and I'll work with you. There's not many kids I'd make this offer to, but you're a good rider with a lot of potential, and you know how to stay out of her way."

It was an *amazing* offer. Sierra knew that. What thirteen-year-old girl ever got an opportunity like this? Then why should it make her feel so awful? She looked at her saddle horn and part of the answer came. *I don't really ride Ladybird. She carries me around while she does her thing. She's just babysitting me! Anyway, she's not Chico.* She opened her mouth, but she couldn't get any words to come.

"If you want to cut on *Chico,*" Misty went on, "you need to put in a lot of hours on him at home. See if you can get him to relax around cattle. I should have seen that earlier; I did, actually–but I wanted to help you, and I thought he'd work out of it quicker."

"Sorry," Sierra whispered.

"No, it's not your fault. But I don't have the time to help him through this, and the only cows I have are the ones I lease from your dad. I've got to keep them fresh for my other riders. You can do it–you've got the ideal setup for pasture training at home. And it's no disgrace to take a horse back to kindergarten. He's a smart boy. He can do this, if you can find the way to teach him."

"Okay." Sierra's voice came out gruff and choky. She twisted her fingers into Chico's black mane. "I guess. I'll, I'll–ride him home now. It's only four miles."

"Sierra." Misty's voice sounded softer. Sierra looked up. "Think hard about this, okay? Just getting Chico ready to start real training could take a while. A year, maybe.

And if the horse you love can't do what you want, or can't do it soon enough–sometimes it makes sense to move on. Ladybird can teach you a lot."

Sierra nodded–she was probably supposed to–and turned Chico down the long driveway toward home.

. . .

CHICO WAS DELIGHTED. FINALLY, SIERRA WAS taking him somewhere again! Down the driveway, down the road. It felt good to move along and see something different.

The fences ended, and Sierra turned him toward the edge of the road and the grassland beyond. There was a tricky-looking ditch. Chico couldn't see how deep it was, and of course, it might be full of snakes. Sierra couldn't make him jump it; she seemed kind of feeble up there anyway, not really in charge. But he didn't want to make trouble. Something seemed off about Sierra. He gave the ditch one last careful look and hopped neatly over it, feet tucked high.

Sierrra pointed him toward–yes! Toward the ranch. Toward the queen. He struck up an energetic lope, and she let him go–and was it raining? No, that was her, dropping warm tears on his shoulders.

Why? He felt wonderful, enjoying his own powerful strides and the steady drumbeat of his hooves, after weeks of chasing laundry back and forth. This must be good for Sierra, too. It had to be.

Maybe it was. She stopped raining on him. Gradually, she seemed to be gathering her strength. Fine. He slowed to a steady jog that he could keep up for a long time. Finally, she reined him in, with a gigantic sniffle. "Oh, Chico. What am I going to do?"

Ahead, Chico saw a fence, and *way* ahead he saw cattle. *Let's go!* he suggested, grabbing more rein. Chasing cows should cheer her up, right? Well, maybe not. That was when she got upset, wasn't it? When he bounced at the cows Randall was working. It was all some kind of game. Chico didn't understand it, but then, the games people thought of never did make a lot of sense to him.

They traveled along the fence line until they came to the gate. Sierra dismounted to open it. She led Chico through, then turned to close it. The reins were draped loosely over her arm, Chico noticed. She wasn't holding them, she wasn't on his back, he was practically home again, and the cattle were close enough that he could smell their sweet dusty aroma. He'd been calm, steady, and levelheaded for a long time, but this was just too much.

Chico whirled on his haunches. Sierra lunged for the reins, but Chico easily outran her. He thundered toward the cattle, stepping on one of his reins. *Ow!* That hurt his mouth. It happened again, and then the reins were gone and he was among the cows, teeth bared, biting backs and tails.

The cows raced away from him at a wild, groaning gallop, toward a nearby clump of pines. They vanished into it and Chico pulled up, aware of an engine sound in the distance. The four-wheeler; he hadn't seen that in a while.

But where was Sierra? He wheeled, head high, wheeled again, and at last, a long way back, a *long* way, he saw a small heap of something. What was that?

He loped toward it and circled warily. A human? It smelled like one. It smelled like Sierra–but he'd never seen a human do this, just collapse on the ground all humped up. She hadn't fallen off; he knew that. And he was sure he hadn't knocked her down. She'd never gotten close enough. But she was crying. That sound he did know. He minced closer, reached gently toward her half-hidden face, and licked her salty cheek.

She raised her head. "Oh, Chico. Oh, you *bad* horse!" She hugged his head; it felt uncomfortable, but Chico decided to let her. Something had just happened that should never happen. He was meant to be steady and reliable, even in the midst of great excitement. Dean and his mother and his whole nature had taught him that. And he'd made Sierra cry.

The engine sound was louder, and there was barking.

Sierra pulled back from Chico and turned her head. "Of *course,*" she whispered. *"Dad."*

The four-wheeler stopped. Dad got off. Sierra stood up to face him.

"You all right?" Dad asked.

"I didn't fall off," Sierra said quickly. "He got away while I was closing the gate."

"I saw," Dad said. "You want to ride him back?" Now *his* voice sounded like Dean's, full of anger and self-control. He opened the toolbox on the four-wheeler and handed Sierra some frayed pieces of baling twine. With shaky fingers, she knotted them to Chico's bit in place of the broken reins.

"Suppertime, we'll talk this over," Dad said. "But I can't have a horse harassing my cattle, Sierra." He drove toward the trees, where the cows had disappeared.

Sierra hauled herself into the saddle without a word. The baling-twine reins felt light and floaty. The loose strands tickled Chico's neck. His mouth hurt from stepping on and breaking his real reins, and now something was even stranger about Sierra. It was like she wasn't really up there. Nothing was coming from her. She was frozen, shut down.

But they were almost home, and then, there was the queen, in the small pasture with cows and calves grazing alongside her. Chico whinnied. She raised her head and after a moment whinnied back. Chico danced. She *did* like him. She actually *liked* him.

. . .

MAYBE SHE WAS THE ONLY ONE WHO DID. ALL evening, while he watched the cows grazing just beyond the corral fence, and the young calves bumbling around, Chico's attention was drawn to the house, to the sound of unhappy voices. Sierra had been upset when he ran away; he'd known that. But he'd thought she would get over it, the way Dean always did.

Sierra wasn't over it. He could tell by the way she behaved when she came out after supper to give him hay. First she acted like he wasn't even there. Then suddenly, she hugged his neck. She didn't say anything–rare for her–but he picked up that same dazed feeling he'd gotten from her earlier.

The sun went down, the stars came out, the moon rose. One by one, the lights went off in the house. No late-night visit from Sierra? She always used to come down and say good night.

The queen crunched hay. Chico didn't feel like eating hay. His mouth still hurt from stepping on his reins, and anyway, he was confused. He listened to the wind in the pines and to the coyotes out there somewhere in the dark.

Closer than usual. Their shrieks and wails tore the nighttime quiet to rags.

Then they fell silent. Chico dozed, slouching on one hip. He still listened, though. Any movement among the cattle brought his ears drowsily forward. Once in a while, he turned to look at the house, but there was no movement there. Nothing at–

There! His head shot up, ears pointing toward a new sound. What was it? The queen stopped chewing. The cattle stirred. Out beyond them something moved. A wild-dog smell, a dried-blood smell, drifted on the night air.

The cattle began to bunch together, calves stumbling up from sleep, mothers nudging them, pushing them, crowding them toward the trees.

Near the horse fence, a calf let out a startled *blat,* and a cow charged into a cluster of gray shapes. A sharp yip–they scattered, then regrouped. The calf staggered toward the horse corral fence. The cow started after it with a low moan, but the shapes were closer. They were on it, pulling it down–

No! No dog-animal had any right to come near territory Chico controlled. He charged. So did the mother cow. The coyotes slipped away. Ignoring Chico, so close on the other side of the fence, the cow lowered her head and gave her calf a worried shove, urging it to move.

The calf tumbled, slithering under the corral fence. On Chico's side, it struggled to rise. Farther along the fence line, a gray shadow slipped under the bottom rail, another, a third.

Chico froze. Not in fear. He would love nothing more than to charge among them with hooves flying, jaws wide-open. He'd get at least one, he knew that.

And the other coyotes would circle–some were behind him even now–and they'd get the calf while he fought them.

It was small. Young.

His!

The calf started to stagger toward the coyotes, in baby stupidity or lack of control. It was very new to the world, and it was hurt. Chico smelled blood on it.

Stop! He closed his teeth gently on its neck. The calf stumbled to its knees, and Chico pushed it all the way down. With one deliberate, careful step, he straddled the calf, snaking his head at the circling shadows. *You think so, dogs? Try it!*

Beyond the fence, the mother cow bellowed. The queen snorted in disgust. She did not appreciate any of this. Chico should be clearing those coyotes out, not just standing there. She trotted by, delivering him a sharp nip in passing, and charged into the cattle pack. They melted away from her, reformed behind, and the mother cow roared. Down by the creek, the rest of the herd answered, and in the house a light came on. In a moment, someone was on the porch. Then running footsteps, bobbing flashlight; Dad, carrying a long stick. He stopped at the fence, pointed the stick toward the sky–

BLAM! The sound was sharp, heavy, unbelievably loud. The queen raced around the perimeter of the corral, snorting. Everything in Chico wanted to do the same. But he held himself still over the calf.

The coyotes vanished. He heard their racing paws for a second. Then all sound was drowned by the mother cow's bawl.

The horse corral was suddenly flooded with light. Dad came back to the fence. Mom and the girls ran from the house.

"What happened?"

"What was it?"

"Strange," Dad said. "I've never known coyotes to bother a horse before. They were all around–Chico, here." He sounded like he could hardly bring himself to say Chico's name.

Sierra scrambled over the rails and came running. "Chico, it's me! Are you okay–oh!" She stopped short. "Dad," she called after a moment. "Come here."

Dad opened the gate and came in. It was the first time Chico had ever seen him in the corral.

"Look under Chico," Sierra said. Dad bent, pointing his flashlight. "It's bleeding," Sierra said. "It's hurt."

"Okay, that's *it*!" Dad sounded so furious, Chico wanted to move away. But there were too many people around him. Mom was coming now, too. Where could he put his feet so he didn't hurt the calf, or any of them?

"End of discussion!" Dad said. "I want this animal off this ranch!"

Mom took the flashlight from him. She put a hand on Chico's neck and bent, shining light on the calf.

"Darling?" she said after a moment. "Take a closer look. Those are coyote bites."

Dad bent and stared where she was pointing. Then he half turned, looking off into the darkness; turned back and looked at Chico and the calf. He opened his mouth. He closed it again.

"Well," he said finally. "Well. He was protecting it, wasn't he?"

Mom nodded.

"I fired a shot from twenty feet away, and this horse didn't move. I'll–I'm–I don't know what to say."

"How about, 'Thank you'?" Mom said.

"Yeah, that one I figured out." Dad held out his hand

toward Chico, palm up. Chico sniffed it. A hard hand, made raspy from work. Awkwardly, gently, the hand stroked Chico's nose.

"Misjudged you, buddy," Dad said. "Admittedly, you've given me plenty of cause, but not this time . . . thanks."

Gently, Mom slid the calf out from between Chico's legs. "This baby needs stitches," she said.

When the calf was out from under him, Chico shook himself, like he would after a nice roll in the dirt. A moment later, Sierra had her arms around his neck.

"Chico, you're *amazing*!"

Chico nibbled gently at her bathrobe tie. She was happy again. Probably some kind of pattern here . . .

. . .

WHILE MOM STITCHED THE CALF UP, AND ADDIE fed both horses an entire bag of carrots, Sierra stood leaning against Chico's shoulder. His warmth came through her pajamas. He ate carrots happily, but a large part of his attention seemed to be out beyond the fences. On the cows? Maybe the coyotes?

"Back to bed," Mom said finally, shooing them all toward the house.

Sierra went to her room, but sleep was impossible. She wrapped her quilt around herself and stared out her bedroom window. She could see Chico in the horse corral, moonlight gleaming butter-yellow on his back. He stood close to the mare, but he looked out toward the calf pasture.

He's a cow horse all right, she thought.

This afternoon, at Misty's, he'd scattered cattle like a gleeful Labrador puppy. That was bad. But tonight, he'd stood over a tiny calf to protect it. That showed judgment. It showed courage. It showed amazing self-control. At supper, Mom had talked about finding him another home, but a horse like Chico shouldn't be a backyard pet or be ridden in slow safe circles in a show ring. He had cow sense, and horse sense, and something almost approaching human sense.

"I'm keeping you," she whispered into the darkness. If Chico couldn't do cutting, she'd do something else with him. He was *hers.*

But when she turned from the window, the Misty Lassiter pictures looked down on her in the dark; shadowy horses facing cattle, Misty riding in all of them.

Sierra went to her bureau and switched on the small light. She looked at herself in the mirror. Gradually her face took on the Lassiter Look–calm, flinty, confident, determined.

Cowboy up, Ranch Girl! He can learn how to cut cattle, if you can find the way to teach him.

CHAPTER 8

ALL THE NEXT DAY, BETWEEN EATING, NAPS, and liniment rubs and hugs from Sierra, Chico watched the wounded calf and its mother. The calf didn't smell of blood anymore. It smelled sweet and grassy from its mother's constant licking. It blundered around stiffly, and the cow kept a sharp watch on it. She watched Chico, too.

The two pens shared a water tub. When the cow came to drink, Chico sauntered closer, picking up wisps of hay from the ground, pretending to pay no attention. The cow wasn't buying it. She tossed her horns and made blowing sounds. Then she drank again.

Chico lifted his nose to the water. He took a couple of swallows, then raised his head. He breathed in the cow's sweet, grassy scent. She looked at him through her thick lashes, and sniffed deeply, too. Then she turned away, but not as if she was frightened.

After dark, when the coyotes sang far out on the grassland, the cow nudged her calf closer to the horse fence. She and Chico stood listening until the shrieks faded.

By morning, the cow stood comfortably near him, washing her calf. Chico stuck his nose through the bars, and the cow turned her head and gave him a swipe with her long, rasping tongue.

Startled, he drew back. But it did feel good. He put his head near again, and the cow began washing his face. Her rhythmic tongue put him into a trance. After a long time, he realized he was being watched. Lazily he turned his head and saw Sierra leaning against the fence. Her eyes were wide, but she didn't say a thing; and Chico turned back to his new friend.

. . .

THIS IS THE HARDEST PART, **SIERRA THOUGHT.** *Calling Misty.*

No, the hardest part was *making* herself call Misty.

She'd lain awake for two nights now, imagining training Chico all by herself. She'd get Dad to loan her some cows. She'd work Chico in the pen with them one at a time, slowly. She'd felt herself riding him, saw the cow framed between his ears–

Then the imaginary cow dodged, or ran, or stopped, and a different part of her brain asked, *Now what?* There were a hundred wrong ways to respond, and only one or two ways that would teach Chico the right thing. She knew enough to know that. Now, watching Chico get a bath from a cow, she was sure he could learn to be calm around cattle. That made it even more important to train him right.

Come on, Ranch Girl! This is your first test.

She brought the phone out to the porch. It was early, but Misty was already on her way to the barn when she answered the call.

"A cow is *licking* his face? I'd like to see a picture of that!" Misty listened to the stories. Chico chasing cows in the afternoon, guarding a calf at midnight, having his face washed by the mother two days later.

There was a short silence when Sierra was done.

"You've committed to this horse, haven't you?" Misty said.

Sierra nodded, and then hastily said, "Yes."

"Good! You'd be a fool not to!"

Sierra sagged with relief. Misty understood.

Misty went on: "One of my mentors used to say, 'Make a cow horse first. Then train a cutting horse, and then see if you can turn him into a competition cutter.' That's old-style pasture training and it hasn't been my approach, because I don't have a ranch full of cattle to play with. You do. Just take him out and fool around near the cows. Whenever he gives you some of his attention around cattle, reward him. Help your dad move stock around with him. And when you think he's ready, call me again."

. . .

THE NEXT DAY SIERRA AND ADDIE, CHICO AND the queen went out into the pasture together. When they came upon a cluster of cows, Sierra walked Chico toward one that stood apart from the rest. He pointed his ears at her. *Chase? Or not?* Somehow it didn't feel as urgent as a couple of days ago. Sierra asked him to stop, just when the cow was considering moving, and he decided to humor her.

"Good!" Sierra leaned down and offered him a nub of carrot.

Chico crunched it, focusing on her for a moment. *More coming?*

They stood. They watched the cow, who did nothing.

Boring. Chico turned his head away, and with a light rein, Sierra tipped his nose back toward the cow. "Good!" And another carrot.

Huh! She wanted him to just *look* at this cow? And she was willing to pay? *Good deal!*

Chico focused, staring hard. The cow's ears flickered and she took a step. Chico started to step toward her. Sierra reined him so he was walking parallel with the cow, mirroring her steps, staying well back. *No chasing. No running. Bizarre.* After a few minutes, when the cow stood still, Sierra dropped her hand on his neck and turned him toward Addie and the queen. Big chunk of carrot. *Weird.*

They walked around the cows in the pasture every day, all week, and then a second week. Chico was getting bored with it. His calf had healed up, and his cow was back with the herd. He wouldn't have minded seeing her again, but cows standing still and eating? This was getting old.

Then one afternoon, Sierra actually rode him through a group of cows. Four walking steps and a carrot chunk. Four more, and another chunk. Through the group and out the other side–carrot chunk–and back again. The carrots and praise divided his mind. Instead of concentrating on cows, he was halfway listening to Sierra.

After a few more days, he started to sense when she was staring at a particular cow. If he stared at it, too, he'd get a carrot–nice, but puzzling, all this approval for going slow.

Now he started to love gliding through a herd, so close he could feel the cows' body heat, hear their stomachs rumble. He loved how they shifted gently out of his way, without haste, without stress. Carrots were cool, too, but not really the point. They were just information that he was making Sierra happy.

He didn't always make her happy, though. Some days, all the serenity got to him, and he couldn't resist a little jump at a cow, just to see her run. There was one day when Sierra got off, gave the reins to Addie, and walked away, turning her back on him. She hugged herself, and yelled, "I can't *do* this!" She stood there for several minutes. But then she came back, and they went for a gallop across the pasture. That was fun, too. Jackrabbits flashed their tails and ran. The aspen leaves quaked in the dry summer wind. Huge white clouds sailed across the sky. It was a big world out here, and there was more to see than just cows.

But cows were still the best.

Another morning–the grass was high now, the sun hot, and the girls didn't have school–Sierra did something new. She rode Chico toward a cluster of four cows at the edge of the group, pressing closer and closer until they walked away from the main herd. Zig, zag, zig–

The cows turned and separated, filtering past Chico toward the larger group. Apparently Sierra was okay with that. She was telling him to let it happen–

No. Not *all* the cattle. She focused on the last one. It tried to pass, and Sierra's leg nudged Chico over into the animal's way.

The cow made a move left. Before Sierra's leg could tell him anything, Chico moved with it. Duck, dodge, block–*yes!* That was the game. The cow wanted back in. He and Sierra kept her out.

Dimly, Chico heard Sierra say, "Good!" But he didn't want a carrot slice, and anyway, there was no time. The cow pressed close. Chico put his ears back, ready to charge–and felt Sierra tell him something unbelievable.

Back up?

He did, telling Sierra with his ears that it was a dumb idea.

Only it wasn't. Suddenly there was room to block the cow again. Somehow it all worked better that way. The cow came to a standstill. Chico felt Sierra's hand on his neck. "*Good* boy! *Good* Chico!" And she hopped off and fed him lots of carrot chunks.

Chico gazed past her at the cattle, eating almost absentmindedly. Something felt so right about what they'd just done. It went way beyond carrots and praise, and the zingy, happy feeling coming off Sierra. He was born for this. He knew it in his bones. It had taken him a long time to understand, but he was here now. In the right place. Doing the right thing.

For the next few weeks, they cut cattle in the pasture every day. Sierra was learning to be helpful, Chico noticed. She picked good cows–lively, smart, interesting ones–and then stayed out of his way as he played with them. She was also starting to melt into the saddle like Misty did, as if they were one. Who moved first or thought first? Who was in charge? Chico didn't care, as long as they both kept learning, as long as the dance went on.

. . .

ONE MORNING IN EARLY AUGUST, DAD ASKED AT breakfast, “Could you and Chico give me a hand today? I need to move some cows up out of the creek bed. It’s got to be done slowly. Is he ready for that?”

“I . . . *think* so,” Sierra said cautiously. “At least, I’m pretty sure I can stop him from being bad.”

“Okay,” Dad said with a smile. “We’ll start with that.”

Later, when they followed Dad out to the creek bed, Sierra saw that a group of cows were making it their home instead of roaming with the herd. She could see the trouble spot–a mud hole, with a broad, trampled triangle leading up out of the water. Several cows grazed under the willows. Others stood in the stream. They looked so peaceful, it seemed sad to disturb them.

But Wyoming grasslands were dry and fragile, and this erosion was ugly, the kind of ugly Dad stayed awake nights worrying about. He loved his land almost as much as he loved his family.

He stopped the four-wheeler and gave Sierra her instructions. “Move them gently up out of the creek bed. Once they’re out, ease way back. Just let them graze along toward the herd. Let ’em think it was their own idea.”

“Won’t they come back?”

“Not if you do it right. Cows go back to where they’ve

felt safe and happy. You're going to *keep* them safe and happy, just moseying across the flat. They'll get even happier when they hit grass that isn't all chewed down. But if you chased them across the flat with a whoop and a holler, they'd think the *flat* was the scary place, and they'd double back just as soon as we were gone. People say cows are dumb," Dad went on, looking at Sierra's puzzled expression. "But they're the best thing there is at being cows. It's up to us to figure them out."

"O-kay." Sierra rode down the slope toward the water. She'd never ridden Chico into a creek before. Would he go?

At the edge, he hesitated, putting his head down to look. One black-tipped ear tilted back at her. She could nudge him on with her heels, or–

No, better idea. She focused her gaze on the nearest cow, standing brisket deep in the flowing water. Immediately, Chico focused on it, too. He minced down into the creek, paying attention to his footing, yet still locked on the cow.

As they got nearer, Sierra switched her focus to the next cow, then past to an open stretch of water. She turned Chico back toward the group, riding purposefully, but slowly.

Like full diners getting up from a restaurant table, the cattle casually turned and lumbered up the bank, bringing a dark, mucky smell out of the water. Chico waded after them. Sierra looked down at the swirling, honey brown reflection of Chico's coat and herself on him and suddenly realized–she was happy. Perfectly, deeply happy. Moving cattle. Helping Dad. Helping the creek, and helping the land. Chico was a cow horse, and–*I'm definitely a ranch girl!*

Up on dry ground, some cattle started grazing. Others headed toward the larger herd off near the trees. Sierra aimed Chico at the lazy ones, getting just inside their bubble–their flight zone, Dad would call it. Chico made a slight suggestion that it would be more fun if they were running, but when she ignored it, he settled into a lazy walk.

The cattle kept moving. Sierra didn't need Dad's hand signal. She faded back, letting the cattle stray across the sunny grassland toward their friends and family. It all felt completely peaceful.

"That horse has come a long way," Dad said, pulling alongside Sierra in the four-wheeler. He'd taken a risk here, Sierra realized, trusting Chico with an important job.

"He really has, hasn't he?"

"Time for you to give Misty a call?" Dad suggested.

"Probably." And so much for peace. A hundred worries blossomed. Would she lose the new, calm Chico–the lazy Chico, ambling after cows? Or was it bad that he'd gotten so calm? Had he lost his edge? What if Sierra had done everything, absolutely everything, wrong?

And there was another question, so big that she didn't want to let herself ask it.

Was competition cutting really what she–and Chico–wanted anymore?

CHAPTER 9

SIERRA PUT OFF MAKING THE CALL TO MISTY. *We're not ready yet,* she told herself.

A few days later, she and Chico helped bring in some young stock from the mountain pasture. They climbed high up the slope, along the cow paths that terraced the steep meadows, searching out small groups of cattle and suggesting gently that they move downhill and through the gate. The first time they'd done this, back in the spring, Chico had pranced and danced and tried to blast through the herd. Now, in late summer, he was a working cow horse, strolling when he could, charging when he had to.

They reached the pen. As Chico walked the cattle through the open gate, Sierra saw Misty leaning against the fence. Misty beckoned with one finger. Sierra rode toward her; heart pounding.

"Ranch Girl," Misty said. "You been holdin' out on me? How long has he been like this?"

"Um–three weeks? A month?"

"What've you been doing with him? Show me your stuff!"

Sierra turned Chico toward the cows. They were unsettled, and she walked him through them until they gathered in a loose bunch near one end of the pen. A group near the edge stuck together, shoving their heads under each other's necks. Sierra rode behind them, focusing. Chico eased them away from the rest.

Once they were beyond the herd, she let two cows filter past and sharpened her gaze on the third. Chico sharpened, too, crouching to meet the nervous heifer's gaze, working her left, right, left. A short run, a stop, and she stood still, letting out a bellow of frustration. Sierra put a hand on Chico's neck, picked up the reins, and turned him toward Misty.

Misty let out a long whistle. She opened the gate to let them out of the pen and closed it behind them. "So," she said. "What's the deal?"

Sierra's hand twisted nervously into Chico's mane. "I–like him like this. I'm not sure–"

"Not sure you want to rev him up again?"

It was partly that, partly wondering if the other students would welcome Chico back. And did she want to play at working cattle when she could *really* work cattle right here at home for real? Too complicated to put into words. She nodded.

"Tell you what," Misty said. "Bring him over. Let's prep him for my youth show in a couple of weeks. You won't win. It's too late for that. But it'll be good experience for both of you–and who knows? Maybe you'll have a good time!"

Sierra doubted that; not if this gnawing feeling in her stomach was any clue. But she found that she couldn't say no.

. . .

THE NEXT MORNING BEFORE SUNRISE, SIERRA came down to the corral–in a mood of some sort, Chico could tell. She saddled and rode him across the pastures, over the ditch and up the road to Misty's.

Pickup trucks were pulling in already, and the place was starting to hum.

Sierra put Chico into his old stall with some hay and disappeared, too tense to say good-bye. Chico didn't eat. Now he was tense, too. Was it all going to start up again? The laundry? The boredom?

After an hour, Sierra came back, more relaxed. She saddled him again and rode him to the indoor arena–and there were his cattle, the same ones he'd brought in from the mountain pasture yesterday.

Sierra rode him toward them and took up a position beside the herd, just like the last time they were in this arena, a couple of months back. Chico remembered his own excitement from that day, bouncing at Randall's cow.

But there were other memories since then, of quietly moving cattle every day, of focusing where Sierra focused.

Right now, Sierra was focused on the whole herd. Well, not entirely. Part of her was worried about the single rider who rode among the cattle and drove a group out. She would look at him, Chico would glance that way, too, and she'd snap her gaze ferociously back to the herd. Chico tried to keep up with her. *Relax. Okay?* He carried his head a little lower than normal, pricked his ears softly, breathed deep.

"If you could be as mellow as your horse, Ranch Girl, you'd have it made!" Misty said. And then Sierra did relax, soften into the saddle, and the day got a lot easier. They held the herd near the back wall for three, four, five cutters. Easy work. *No sweat.* Chico could do it with his eyes shut.

In the afternoon, Sierra rode him home. She was relaxed, exhausted, gleeful. She kept patting him, and when she got off at the gate, she hugged him. A long day, a good day, and there was grain for supper.

Next day, they went to Misty's again. This time Chico was a turn-back horse. That was harder. Sierra focused on each cow as if she were cutting it, and Chico focused too. As a turn-back horse, he knew now that he wasn't supposed to go head to head with the cow. He was supposed to make the heifer turn *away* from him and back toward the cutter. Sierra never once put her hand down and turned things over to him. Still, it was fun. Anytime he got to control a cow was fun.

The third day, Chico got to be the cutter a few times. Misty had a lot to say, and he felt Sierra listening carefully. She used her legs to guide him more. She didn't seem to know as much as he did about what the cow was going to do, but Chico obeyed her, and a cow got away from him. How could that happen?

Then it happened again.

"You're trying too hard, Ranch Girl!" Misty said. "Easy does it!"

Sierra stopped using her legs as much. *Good!* Chico didn't mind her input in setting up the cut. She knew how to pick a fun cow. But leave the rest to him! *He* was the one who knew what the cow would do next.

A couple of weeks like this, with here and there a day of rest. As long as there were cows, it was all good for Chico, though maybe somewhat pointless now. At home, there was a job, they did it, and then they did something else. Here the job was always the same and never done. And Sierra wasn't perfectly settled, though everyone was friendlier to her than in the spring. The other riders asked her questions, usually about cows, and she asked them questions in return. And laughed sometimes, and sometimes made them laugh. But she had something else on her mind. Chico could tell that, but he didn't know what.

One day, new cattle arrived, strange cattle. Chico didn't see them, but he could tell by the bellows and the smell. New horses came, too, and new riders. The whole place was in a bustle. That afternoon, Sierra didn't ride Chico home. She left him in the stall. He almost didn't want his hay, he was so concerned about that. *Almost.*

Early the next morning, Sierra came back, with Mom, Dad, and Addie. She was nervous. Chico was, too, with all the bustle of strange horses, strange riders, and strange cattle. He kept an ear cocked as Sierra brushed him, and suddenly he heard a voice he knew. His head swiveled. A deep nicker burst from his throat. *Dean!*

"Hey, buddy!" Dean said. "I'm glad to see you, too!"

Chico put his nose to Dean's cheek and inhaled the familiar scent. He smelled faint traces of his mother and the rest of the herd, of the neighborhood, real laundry, backyard flowers. But mostly it was just Dean, the first human he'd ever known, his friend.

Dean reached into his pocket and brought out–yes, a gingersnap. He was the only person who had ever given Chico a gingersnap. Chico crunched it, and Dean stepped back. After a moment, he whistled. "He looks great! Look at those muscles! "

"We're very happy with him," Mom said. "In fact, I wonder if you'd consider parting with one of his brothers next spring. That bay, the quiet one?"

"Oh!" Dean stroked his chin, nodding thoughtfully.

Chico watched him for a moment, then looked around. Where was Sierra? Oh, good–coming with the saddle. He was happy to see Dean, but Sierra was his person now, the one he belonged with.

. . .

SIERRA FELT JANGLED. HER WHOLE FAMILY WAS supporting her as if competition cutting were her lifelong dream–which it used to be, but was it anymore? Chico was a cow horse already, a horse with a purpose.

Would he be good today? Would he stay calm? *I just want him not to disgrace us!* Sierra thought. *Though wouldn't it be amazing if we won? But he couldn't possibly–*

"Breathe, Ranch Girl!" Misty said. She was everywhere at once this morning.

Sierra made a gulping sound.

Misty said, "Listen–a pasture-trained horse like Chico is apt to figure out that he doesn't have to do some of the stuff we do in competition. I want to keep it real for him. So get saddled and get over to the arena. I want you to settle the herd."

Sierra gasped. "You want *Chico*–"

Misty grinned. "Amazing but true!" She strode on, showering words of encouragement everywhere.

In a daze, Sierra saddled up. Settling the herd was one of the most important jobs at a contest. These were new cattle. They'd never been used for cutting before. The settler's job was to make the herd feel safe near the fence, then drive them gently into the middle and show them that they could get back to the fence; get them used to being moved around by a horse. Show management–in this case, Misty–picked the settler, and it was a mark of trust in both rider and horse.

Chico had been doing this same kind of work all summer, with no helpers and no walls, just miles of open air and grass. He'd done it at the creek bed, and bringing the new cows in. This was a real job, an important job. Done right, it would make the competition better for everyone. Was Chico up to the task in the arena, in front of a crowd, with this buzz of excitement?

Was she?

. . .

WHAT WAS THE MATTER WITH SIERRA? **CHICO** wondered. She kept taking deep breaths, but they weren't relaxing her.

Misty waved from the doorway of the arena, and Sierra *stopped* breathing. Chico was having qualms about going in there, too. The building sounded buzzy, like a nest of bees. It didn't sound safe. But Sierra wanted them to go in, or so she claimed. With a flutter in his stomach, he danced through the door.

Oh! There were a lot of people. They were everywhere, on high seats along the walls. What did they want? Why were they here?

The gate opened at the far end, and Chico saw the strange cows he'd been sensing. They were a kind of cow he'd never seen before: slender, gray, with long ears and slight humps on their shoulders. They clung to each other, more so than the brawny animals he was used to. And they were nervous, quite nervous, milling and shoving each other, trying to not be here.

Suddenly, Chico felt perfectly calm.

Sierra asked him to walk back and forth in front of the cows. Back and forth. Soon the herd loosened up and finally stood quietly. Sierra calmed down, too.

She asked Chico to walk behind the cows–slowly, so slowly. The silky gray heifers bunched together, all walking toward the center of the arena. Chico strolled after them, drawing in their scent in quick, puffing breaths. Young cows. Scared cows. Fast cows.

"Whoa," Sierra said softly. Chico stood, watching the herd. Then Sierra nodded to the other riders, asking them to move forward.

The cattle turned. Chico wanted to step toward them, but Sierra asked him to stand still. The cattle divided, passed on both sides of him, and clustered together at the fence.

Now Sierra rode Chico through the herd, just as she used to in the pasture. Left to right, bringing half of them out and letting them drift back again. Right to left–one cow broke into a run, and Chico leaped to block her, turn her, get her walking with the group again. And right to left through the herd. Left to right . . . they felt calm to him now.

Sierra loped him back and forth in front of the cows a few times. Then she rode toward the gate, and the boy Randall rode in, with three helpers.

"Ride turn-back for me?" Randall asked Sierra. "I was going to ask earlier, but you got tapped to be settler."

"Sure," Sierra said, as calmly as if cute boys always asked her to do important jobs. He should have asked her earlier; that was cutting etiquette. But she *had* been busy.

She turned Chico around beside Randall to look over the cows, as his herd holders moved into position. The other turn-back rider was a girl from Laramie, Tory, who was starting to be Sierra's friend.

"Which cow would you guys pick?" Randall asked.

"Don't look at me!" Tory said. "Ask Sierra. She knows how to pick a cow."

Sierra turned red. "I don't know–the Brahmans aren't my breed. They all look alike to me." But already she was starting to see a few differences. "I'd leave that dark one alone, I know that."

"Really? I kinda like how she looks." Randall waited for her to say more, but Sierra didn't know how to put it. He shrugged, glanced at the judge's booth, and rode forward, holding his rein hand high. Tory and Sierra rode a few steps behind him.

Randall crossed the starting line and eased his horse into the herd, hunting among the cattle. Sierra saw him sift the dark heifer out and discard her. Wow! He was actually taking her advice!

But the dark one pushed into his path again and was among the small group he eased out. Cattle began filtering back around him toward the herd; Sierra stepped Chico toward them, moving them along–*uh-oh!* Randall had chosen the dark heifer after all, or she had chosen him. There was going to be trouble.

Sure enough, the dark cow was wild, a fence-to-fence runner. She refused to turn, to honor the horse, or to make a serious try to get back into the herd. Sierra had to jump Chico into her way several times, and she could feel him starting to get excited. *Quit already!* She thought at Randall. Don't wear us all out on a bad cow.

Eventually, *eventually,* he figured that out and found his chance to quit. Sierra moved into position to escort the dark Brahman out of his way.

Randall glanced at her. “Which one, Ranch Girl?” he asked quietly.

She didn’t want to be obvious about telling him; this was supposed to be his run. Keeping her Lassiter Look firmly in place, she pointed her chin at a plump, pearl-colored heifer at the edge of the herd–then glanced away quickly before Chico could follow her focus.

Randall needed to work on *his* Lassiter Look. His surprise was obvious. But he’d already wasted a lot of his two and a half minutes. Delicately, he peeled Plump Pearl off the edge, got her in position, and started to work her.

As Sierra had expected, she was a gem–the greedy ones often were–bright-eyed, self-confident, willing to honor a horse, and she had an unexpected turn of speed. Given a good cow, Randall and his horse put on a nice show, and were well started on their third cut when the buzzer sounded.

They turned to ride out together. “Thanks,” Randall said. “Wish I’d listened to you the first time–well, I did listen, but she was right there, all framed up, and you know how it is. When one cow’s a little different than the others, isn’t that the one you pick every time?”

"That's a guy thing, Randall!" Tory said.

Sierra didn't think so. She'd seen lots of riders pick a cow with odd markings or a different coloration. It wasn't always a good cow; or not one she'd pick herself. But, as a ranch girl, she knew cattle–and that gave her an advantage in cutting.

Which sounded like she was staying in the game, didn't it?

Outside the arena Randall got off and loosened his girth.

"Will you–ride for me?" Sierra asked quickly, before he could disappear to take care of his horse. "I'm Number Eight."

"Sure! I won't give you any advice about cows, though!"

When he was out of earshot, Tory said, "I like the boys in cutting. They tend to be nicer."

"And smarter!" Sierra added.

" 'All you got to be is smarter than a cow!' " Tory went on. "That's what Misty says."

" 'Cows are smarter than you think.' " Sierra answered. "That's what my dad says!"

. . .

THREE TIMES CHICO WALKED INTO THE ARENA, and helped Sierra turn cows back toward the cutter. The energy was high in the arena. He was starting to feel on tiptoes, ready for a little action.

The fourth time they walked in he was slightly in the lead–and yes! It was his turn! Holding the reins high, Sierra rode him toward the herd of mouse-colored heifers and into their midst.

It was hard to make way among them. They were so clingy, afraid of being separated from each other. Many had been worked already, and those cows kept diving back toward the wall. Chico listened for the light touch of the reins on his neck and for Sierra's focus–which was a little lacking. *Hey! Pay attention! Never mind the people!*

He helped her loosen up a group of cows and move them to the center. They started filtering back to the herd, encouraged by the turn-back riders. But Sierra was distracted, scattered. Chico tossed his head, ears flat. *C'mon! Get with the progam!*

Sierra gasped. Good! She was back with him, eyeing the cows, selecting, sifting–

Committed.

The reins fell loose. The extra cattle drifted away, and Chico found himself eye to eye with a shocked gray heifer.

She made a dash–oh, good, a lively one! Chico pounced, came level with the heifer's head, and dropped to a crouch as she stopped. She dashed the other way.

Oh no, you don't!

A smart cow. She dodged and ducked, and Chico mirrored her every move, ears and eyes and every possible sense locked onto her until, with a moan of desperation, she wheeled toward the turn-back riders. What an intense cow!

The second one was a dud. It made a few short dashes, as imaginative as the laundry. Chico was glad to quit that one and turn back to the herd, chip off another heifer from the outside and begin maneuvering–

The buzzer droned. Claps, whistles–oh yeah! There were people out there.

But more important was Sierra's hand on his neck, warm and grateful and full of zing. "Wow! Chico, that was amazing."

And it was over. They walked out of the arena with the other riders, and Sierra hopped off. A hug around the neck, a chunk of carrot. Then she loosened Chico's girth.

Phew! That felt good. There was Mom with a hug for each of them, Dean with another gingersnap, Dad with a water bucket, and Addie chirping, "Chico, Chico!"

A strange voice said, "I don't suppose you'd consider selling him?"

Misty's voice cut in. "Don't be ridiculous! Of course she wouldn't sell him." She gave Chico a friendly clap on the neck and turned to look at Sierra. "What do you think,

Ranch Girl? You want to do competition cutting with this horse?"

Sierra's eyes were wide and bright, looking off into the future. Slowly she nodded, and nodded again.

"I want to do *everything* with him," she said.

CHAPTER 10

THE DAYS WERE CRISP AND FROSTY NOW. THE girls had school again. Afternoons, they hurried to the horse corral to saddle up for a ride. By the time they got back, the shadows of the pines were long across the brown grass.

The calves were fat and furry now. The cattle ate urgently, fattening up for winter. There was still good in the grass, despite its color, and they all felt hungry.

Chico's own sides were thick with new hair. Once in a while, a warm day came, and he and the queen sweated, standing in the paddock. Chico could smell the fragrant hay in the barn. He could smell the spicy leaves on the mountains. Beyond that, he sensed the cold, a way off, but coming.

On weekends, Sierra sometimes rode him over to Misty's to work with the laundry, and sometimes with goats. Chico liked goats; their bleating amused him, and they were much less predictable than cattle. Lots of times, he couldn't tell what a goat would do next. The deep connection wasn't there the same way for him as it was with cattle–but it made for a better game. And, no doubt about it, he liked the game. He belonged here now, as much as he belonged on the ranch. People stopped to watch his training sessions. He was somebody.

Back home, he was somebody, too; a partner, as important as the four-wheeler and the the dog, or the queen.

One evening, a raw wind picked up. The horses stood with their backs to it all night. In the morning, it was still blowing, and big clouds swirled over the mountains northward. Chico smelled snow.

Dad and Sierra came down to the corral together, bundled in thick coats. Sierra got Chico ready. Then she and Dad stood with their breath making white puffs on the air and looked at the mountain.

"The weather service says we have about twelve hours before it hits," Dad said. "But I don't trust that. They've been wrong already about this storm. We have to move fast. I'll take the lower sections, and you comb the high pasture. But, Sierra, listen to me."

His voice sounded so serious that even Chico pricked his ears up, as Sierra turned her head to look at him.

"When you see the first snowflake," Dad said, "I mean it, the *very first*–you turn around with the cows you've got and get off that mountain. Okay? If you aren't back at the gate by the time the ground's white, I'm calling in mountain rescue. We're talking helicopters, dogs, the whole nine yards. You will not believe how embarrassed you'll be!"

"But the cows–"

"Will be snowed in up there. Probably we'll be able to get them off the mountain in a week or so. If not–then we'll lose some. That's the hazard of being a rancher, and it's the hazard of being a cow. The first snowflake, Sierra!" He pointed his gloved finger at her, and she nodded.

They set out; Dad and dog on the four-wheeler, Sierra and Chico trailing behind. Dad opened the gate to the mountain pasture and got his grain bucket out of the back. He shook it; what an appetizing sound!

"Give Chico a handful," Sierra said.

Dad held out his hand, mounded with molasses-sweet grain. Chico was still crunching as Sierra turned him toward the trail.

Up they went, higher and higher. Usually they would meet cattle, but there were none today. The air was raw and burned Chico's lungs. The wind made him feel jumpy. Things looked different on a windy day. *Was* that actually a rock, or some kind of animal giving him the hairy eyeball?

Sierra paid no attention to that. She focused the way

she did in a herd of cattle–but there were no cattle. Were there? Chico didn't see any, or hear them. In fact, the whole mountainside pasture seemed oddly empty.

"Maybe they were all smart and headed downhill," Sierra said. "Come on, let's try this trail." She turned Chico toward a large boulder. A narrow trail led past it. *Intriguing.* Chico liked trails. But . . .

No. Ignoring the reins, he turned his head and then his whole body and looked in the opposite direction, across the mountainside. If it was cattle she wanted–and it usually was–then they should go *this* way. He couldn't see or hear cows and he couldn't really smell them either–but he could *almost* smell them, off toward those trees.

Sierra turned him back toward the boulder and the trail. As politely as he could, Chico kept on turning, full circle, and pointed his ears toward the grove of trees.

"Chico!" Sierra said.

Then she stopped and drew a deep breath. "Okay," she said. "You're the cow horse. We'll try it your way. *Brr!*" Chico heard a *zip* as she snugged her zipper up.

The going across the mountainside was steep and uneven, until Chico's feet suddenly found a narrow trail, a cow path. Now, though the wind blew the scent around and filled his mind with the idea of snow, he could tell that cattle had traveled this way recently. He walked carefully, fitting his feet into the path, pricking his ears thoughtfully and sampling the air with light, fluttery snorts.

Something tickled his ear. Something else tickled his neck.

"Uh-oh! Snow!"

Sierra asked him to stop and looked, first uphill and then down. Chico had been able to hear Dad's voice and the sound of barking for a long time, but not any longer.

More tickles. Snowflakes caught on Chico's eyelashes, blurring his vision.

"We'd better turn around," Sierra said. "I hope the cows will be okay." She picked up the reins. Chico turned gladly on the tiny trail. He'd had enough of this cold mountainside.

But as his head swept around, Chico caught a glimpse of something. He froze, staring. There, among the dark branches of the black pines, he saw a flash of red and white. Cattle, huddled and shoving against each other, and one heifer at the edge of the herd, staring back at him.

Sierra nudged him with her legs. Instead of obeying, he snatched at the reins, turning back, jerking his nose toward them. *There! Cows!*

Sierra looked where he was looking and stiffened in the saddle. Chico couldn't tell what she wanted to do. Go back to them? Keep heading downhill? Snowflakes hissed around them, bending down the goldenrod stalks.

She seemed to reach some kind of decision. "I don't care, we can't leave them, Chico. Not when we're this close. C'mon!"

Slipping on the slender track, Chico trotted toward the cows. Now he could see them clearly, a group of eight or ten huddled within a grove of trees. Sierra turned him aside from the path. He didn't get that for a moment, and then he understood. She wanted to come in behind them.

He climbed the steep rocky slope, slipping, struggling. Then he was above the cows, and she turned him back downhill again. He braced, sliding down on his haunches in a cloud of steaming breath and swirling snowflakes. The cows whooshed their breath and trotted out from under the trees.

Sierra's hand on the reins asked him to pause. The first cow found the path. The others fell in behind it, single file. When they'd gotten well underway, Sierra let Chico follow, back toward the main trail. He could hear Dad calling now, but he wasn't sure Sierra could. Humans had very limited senses–

Far ahead, the lead cow was turning uphill. "Don't you dare!" Sierra gasped.

She clapped her legs against Chico's sides. He blasted

across the hillside, snow and dirt flying, and slammed to a stop in front of the cow. The others fanned toward the main trail and started walking quickly downhill. The former leader slung her head in the air defiantly, but turned and followed the rest.

"Good, Chico!" Sierra said.

She hunched her coat tighter around her. Chico angled his ears to the sides to keep the snow out. They followed the cows, down through the belt of trees, toward the sound of barking and the motor and–

Here came Dad, blasting up the trail; the four-wheeler's engine was really working hard. He pulled his vehicle aside when he saw the cows, and they hurried past him. Now that they'd gotten started, they seemed to know just what to do. There was no need to even drive them through the gate. They hustled through on their own, toward the sheltered lower pastures.

Dad pulled up to shut the gate. The dog hopped onto the seat and flattened his ears briefly at Chico. *Good job, horse.*

"Good work, you two," Dad said.

Sierra didn't say anything, just put her gloved hand on Chico's neck. He felt that zing coming off her, and he knew why. They'd done a big job, he and Sierra, the job they were born for. Cutting was a blast, but this was the real thing. He felt full of fizz, too, and the snowflakes tickled, and he couldn't help prancing. *Let's go! Let's move!*

"All done, Dad?" Sierra asked. "Okay, we're out of here!" With a wild whoop, she slackened the reins.

All right! Chico exploded into a gallop, across the snowy pasture toward home.

Cutting and the American Quarter Horse

The quarter horse is the most popular breed in the world, with more than 4 million registered worldwide. Approximately one third of the 9.2 million horses in the United States are quarter horses.

The breed originated on the East Coast of the American colonies, from Rhode Island, south. The English settlers were passionate about horse racing, but it was too much work to create a standard racecourse in the wilderness. The settlers scraped out quarter-mile tracks–sometimes it was the main street of the village–and ran short races. This favored explosive speed rather than the staying power of the English thoroughbred. The colonists called their racehorses “short horses, “quarter-milers,” or “quarter-pathers.”

The original horses were Spanish barbs, crossed with free-roaming horses of Spanish origin, some wild and some bred by the Chickasaw nation. The barbs spread from a Spanish colony in Florida. Thoroughbred stallions imported after 1750 added more speed and endurance.

When distance racing became popular in the 1800s, the

quarter-pathers went out of fashion as racehorses. Always good-tempered and versatile, they moved west with white settlers, pulling buggies and even plows.

As cattle ranching rose in importance, Western settlers discovered the great talent of their horses. Thanks to their Spanish blood, they had excellent "cow sense" and the speed and agility to perform well as ranch horses. That kindness, athleticism, and cow sense make quarter horses the world's premier Western sport horse.

Quarter horses still race on quarter-mile tracks today. They're the horse of choice for chariot and cutter racing, barrel racing, cowboy mounted shooting, reining, roping, and cutting. They also compete in English sports like dressage, eventing, jumping, and even driving.

American quarter ponies (like Queenie) have been bred since the 1960s. They are an 11.2 to 14.2 hand-high version of the American quarter horse, sturdy and substantial animals with the same agility and cow sense as quarter horses.

The sport of cutting is dominated by quarter horses. Cutting is based on ranch work. Cowboys always needed to bring individual cows out of the herd, for branding, for administering medicines to, or for separating animals to be sold. Horses with a special talent for doing this were much admired. Contests were often set up, with differing formats.

In 1946, the National Cutting Horse Association was organized by thirteen ranchers and cowboys at the Fort Worth

Stock Show & Rodeo. The organization is now active in all fifty states and twenty-two foreign countries.

Each cutting contestant has two and a half minutes to cut at least two cows from the herd. One cow must be brought out from deep inside the herd. The other cuts may be chipped from the edge of the herd.

The contestant has four riders of her choice to help. Two are herd holders, positioned on either side of the herd to keep the cattle from drifting into the middle of the arena. Two more riders stay between the cow being worked and the judges' stands. These are the turn-back riders; they turn the cow back to the cutter if it tries to escape.

When the cutter has separated one cow from the herd, she must *give the horse his head;* it is now the horse's job to hold the cow and keep it from rejoining the herd.

A cutting horse must be calm among cattle, yet capable of explosive bursts of speed and the ability to dominate cattle. Horses with Spanish ancestry, like quarter horses, are particularly apt to have "cow sense." This is due to centuries of driving and working cattle on the Spanish plains, and also to the sport of bullfighting, which makes cow sense a matter of life and death.

American quarter horses are naturals for cutting, but other breeds do well, too; paints, Appaloosas, Morgans, and mustangs have all excelled at cutting.

Like all sports, cutting has its own jargon. Here are a few frequently used terms:

Baldie: white-faced cow

Commit: show intention to work a specific cow by looking at it and stepping toward it

Cow sense: the horse's natural instinct for anticipating a cow's moves

Cowy: showing cow sense and enthusiasm for working cattle

Cutter's slump: posture of cutting-horse riders when they are sitting deep in the saddle. The rider sits on his back pockets with his back relaxed and curved slightly forward.

Drop on a cow: crouching posture of the horse when a cow has been cut and separated, and the rider drops his rein hand on the horse's neck

Help: herd holders and turn-back riders. Asking someone to be a herd holder or turn-back rider at a competiton is referred to as "hiring help," though no money changes hands.

Honor: refers to a cow that will acknowledge and look at a horse and rider

Quit: stop working a cow

Western: a description Western riders use for unruly behavior in a horse

For more information, go to the National Cutting Horse Association Web site.

American Quarter Horse Association: www.aqha.com

National Cutting Horse Association: www.nchacutting.com

JESSIE HAAS has raised and trained three horses, starting with Josey when she was in seventh grade. The author of over thirty books, she has been called "the current queen" of children's horse stories (*BCCB*, April 2004). *Unbroken* won the Parents' Choice Award, *Horse Crazy!* won the American Horse Publications Award, and *Jigsaw Pony* is a Gryphon Award Honor Book. Jessie lives in southern Vermont with her husband, writer Michael J. Daley, two cats, a dog, and a hen, and is currently training a Morgan mare named Robin. www.jessiehaas.com